What they say about Norm's books

"I loved this book, fangs and all." ~Best selling author James Rollins

"... an amusing teen vampire tale..." ~~Five starred review, Harriet Klausner, Amazon's #1 book reviewer on Fang Face

"… humorous fantasy at its best…" ~~ Armchair Interviews (Amazon Top reviewer), on The Adventures of Guy

"No topic is safe from Cowie's incredible wit and entertaining turn-of-phrase." Pop Syndicate (The Adventures of Guy named one of Pop Syndicate's Top Ten Books of 2007)

The Next Adventures of Guy voted
Winner of Preditors and Editors Readers Choice Award for best Sci-Fi Fantasy

"...hilarious mishaps...." Joliet Herald News

"Hilarious, witty and oozing with snappy sarcasm…" 3Rs Bits, Bites & Books on The Adventures of Guy

"Don't bother picking up this one if you've no sense of humor" Amanda Richards, Amazon Top Reviewer

"Everything in the book is so true, you can't help but laugh in agreement." Roundtable Reviews

"…LOL funny" Beverly at Publisher's Weekly

"… profound, funny and persistently entertaining read from first page to last." Midwest Book Review on The Adventures of Guy

"… fantastically funny." BookLoons on Fang Face

"This book sucks ... in a most delightful way. Don't miss this gem.." Shane Gericke, national bestselling author

DEDICATION

This book is dedicated to my family...

... and coffee.

... and platypuses everywhere.

This is a most likely a work of fiction.
But who knows?
Record keeping back then was kind of spotty.

Bonk and Hedz
a caveman ... and woman ... story

Way after Adam and Eve, but still a long time ago.

"Are you ready?" Hedz asked, peering at her mate.

Her dark brown eyes were deep-set under a thick ridge of bone from which sprouted a thick unibrow that looked like a sleeping ferret. She was naked, stringy and dark-skinned, with a forehead sloping steeply backward to disappear into a tangled mass of thick unwashed hair. Her single most outstanding feature was a fantastic, flowing mustache Hulk Hogan would have coveted.

In short, Hedz was a magnificent looking cavewoman.

Bonk looked a lot like his mate, with the exception that his body parts were male, and his moustache wasn't quite as remarkable. There was another difference. He had a jagged scar on his forehead, a direct result of being a tall caveman in a short cave. The scar was shaped like a lighting bolt, but as far as he knew it gave him no special powers.

They were crouching on a small hill overlooking the river. A log had fallen into the river and several turtles had climbed on top to sun themselves. Bonk and Hedz were hoping to sneak down on the vigilant reptiles and snatch one or two before they could slide into the safety of the water.

Bonk shifted uncomfortably. "I dunno. I don't know how I feel about you helping. After all, I'm the hunter and you're just a gatherer."

5

Hedz simply gave him a look, which he neatly avoided by turning his gaze back down to their quarry down by the riverbank.

"Okay, let's go." Hedz slipped down the hill into the messy brush that grew lush from roots dipping into the river. She crept through the undergrowth, her clever feet making no noise as she deftly avoided fallen branches and dead crunchy leaves. Bonk followed, crackling and crunching as he was unable to duplicate his mate's stealth.

The turtles started shifting and a few lazily opened their eyes, slightly more alert. With the crocs in the river and all manner of predator on land, it wouldn't take much for them to dive into the safety of the shallows.

Hedz froze, her eyes intent on the turtles.

After a tense moment, the sun warmed them back into somnolence.

Hedz waited for a moment to see if the turtles were faking, and then she resumed her ninja approach. When they were six feet away from the water's edge, they stopped again.

"Okay, here's where we really have to be quiet," Hedz said, her lips moving without sound.

"What?" Bonk asked.

Hedz quickly clamped a hand over his mouth. "Quiet," she mouthed.

He nodded.

Her gaze went back to the turtles which were still on the log. Their eyes were open, but fortunately their attention was on the water rather than the shore.

After a moment, the turtles' eyelids drooped.

"Let's go," Hedz whispered.

They crept through the last bit of brush. As Bonk followed his mate, something grabbed his long hair, yanking him backward.

"Oorgh," he gasped.

He tried to turn to see what had him, but a low hanging branch reached down to snag his wild mane.

"Augh."

He spun around, long tendrils of hair wrapping around his torso and catching on prickly thickets.

"Uuuf."

More hair was snatched by grabby branches and a tentacle of hair tightened around his knees. He tottered wildly.

"Aaagh."

The turtles' beady eyes snapped open.

"Shhh!" Hedz hissed.

"Umph," Bonk replied.

He tried to move, but the hair wrapped around his legs tightened and he crashed to the ground.

Hedz watched in dismay as the turtles slipped into the water like Olympic lugers. As the water swallowed them, she whirled around. "What the heck is the matter..."

Words escaped her at the site of her mate completely entangled in branches, vines and his own hair.

"Mpfh," he said helplessly, hair wrapped around his mouth like a furry python.

"That's it," Hedz snapped. "I'm tired of that stuff."

She roughly tore him from the spider web of hair and branches and dragged him through the brush to a clearing dwarfed by a large pine tree.

"Hold the tree," she commanded.

Tentatively, he wrapped his arms around it.

"Harder."

He tightened his grip, his face smushed up against rough bark.

"Okay, here goes." Hedz took a handful of Bonk's long thatchy hair. She paused, "Are you ready?"

He whimpered. "What are you going to do?"

"Just hold on tight."

He nodded and closed his eyes.

Hedz braced herself and gave a tremendous yank.

"Aaagh!" Bonk yelped as his head was wrenched backward by the powerful cavewoman. She immediately let go, and his head bounced back, scraping painfully on the trunk.

Bonk opened pain-filled eyes. "Did it work?"

Hedz shook her head.

Still dazed, Bonk watched some birds in the sky, idly wondering if they were just circling his head.

Wordlessly, Hedz looked around until she spied a pelican skull on the ground. She picked it up and fed a length of his hair into the beak. Then she chopped as if she were using pruning shears. After a moment, she critically examined the result.

"Darn," she said dolefully.

Bonk grimaced. "What?"

Hedz blew out an exasperated puff of air, "Well, we can't cut it and we can't pull it out. I guess we'll just have to wait until someone invents scissors."

Chapter 1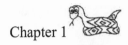

The next morning, Bonk strolled down a path lined with trees on one side and the slow moving croc-filled river on the other. He was carrying a long straight pole made of a branch stripped of leaves. Its end was sharp, jagged and splintered ... and pretty much the most advanced weaponry in the world.

Bonk's attention was on a heron standing in the shallow water. Strolling around admiring wildlife wasn't a good habit to get into, because there were plenty of nasties around ready to gobble a distracted caveman for a snack. But Bonk liked to study wildlife hunting techniques in the hopes he might pick up some pointers, the sad fact being he needed every pointer he could get.

As he watched, the leggy bird neatly speared a fish and gobbled it down. Silently, a set of eyes floated along the river towards the heron. The crafty bird noticed and gracefully launched into the sky. The croc-eyes simply veered downstream to go look for less vigilant prey.

Reminded of the presence of everyday danger, Bonk looked around. Nothing was paying any particular attention to him except for a mosquito which was sucking in some of Bonk's inner juices. He smacked the bug and headed home.

Bonk's cave was located halfway up a steep embankment at the end of a small mountain range. The side of the hill was dotted with caves filled with cavemen, cavewomen, cave-offspring and a host of bugs that depended on them for meals. Further down the range, a small volcano belched out the occasional bit of smoke.

Bonk scrabbled up the loose shale to the cave's mouth and entered the dark, damp opening.

"Close the door," Hedz called as he passed the threshold.

Bonk stopped short, "Door?"

A look went across his mate's face. "Oh, right. We don't have doors yet."

"Yeah, right," Bonk said, as usual having no idea what she was talking about.

As his eyes adjusted to the gloom, he could pick out details. Hedz was nursing Baby Eff in the sleeping pit. Their sons Frigg and Bush were sprawled in another pit that had been dug out and filled with comfortable pebbles. Lump, an ancient woman, was watching with half-lidded interest. They knew little about the old lady who had come with the cave when they moved in. She didn't eat much, said even less and was soon a part of the family. There was no sign of Eff's older sister Gop. He vaguely remembered her talking about a something she called a sleepover.

The boys' eyes were glued to a large rock.

"What are you guys watching?"

(The use of the word 'guy' is a particularly loose translation since the word 'guy' wouldn't be invented until some guy named Guy Fawkes tried to blow up the English Parliament.)

Bush's eyes never left the rock. "We're watching the fights."

Bonk's eyes lit up. "Oh, yeah, who's fighting?"

"Centipede," Frigg grunted.

Now Bonk could see the multi-legged creature crawling over the top part of the rock. It was huge and black, with twitchy antennae, clicking mandibles and a big fat stinger glistening with poison.

"Who's he fighting?"

"Scorpion," Bush replied, popping something into his mouth without looking. Bonk saw a turtle shell filled with munchies in his lap. The munchies were moving. Most likely they were grubs Bush had dug out from under a log.

Just then a large scorpion scuttled from the other side of the rock. The centipede and scorpion spied each other the same time and paused to allow their tiny minds to assess the threat - which didn't take much time, because with such little brains there wasn't much to think with. Coming to the same conclusion at the same time, they rushed each other, claws and fangs flashing.

"Woo-hoo!" Frigg exclaimed.

"Get-em!" Bush roared.

"Boo-ya!" Bonk yelled.

They hooted and hollered as the scorpion and centipede writhed, small drips of poison spit flying through the air.

Hedz's voice cut through the room. "Actually, Frigg and Bush are in trouble. They aren't supposed to be watching any rock right now."

Uh, oh, when she used that tone.

Bonk tore his eyes from the fight. "Why not?" Then he noticed what his mate was wearing and his eyebrows shot up into what little he had of a forehead.

"What are you wearing?"

She grinned, showing sharp canines, "Oh, do you like it?"

"You're, you're, you're wearing …" he stammered.

She supplied the word to him. "Beaver."

"But, but we're naked. We don't wear anything! What you're wearing … it's … it's .. indecent."

Hedz preened. "No, it's provocative. You just don't know the difference."

Lump spoke from the depths of the cave, laughter in her tone, "You're trouble, girl."

Hedz grinned, "I know, right?"

Actually, much to Bonk's surprise, the beaver pelts were turning him on. That and her sexy moustache, which was the envy of all of his friends from the Portsbar. If it wasn't for baby Eff in her arms …

At that moment, the boys roared, slapping their hands on the cave floor in excitement. "Look! He got him!"

As Bonk's head whipped around, his mate's 'ahem' stopped him in mid-whip, causing a mild case of whiplash that any injury attorney would drool over.

"Wha…"

Her eyes were those of a cave lion. "I said they aren't supposed to be watching rock right now."

Her voice was much like that of aforesaid cave lion.

"Why not?" Bonk asked.

She gestured to the wall behind her. "Look, they drew graffiti all over the wall again."

She was right. The wall was filled with crudely drawn antelopes running from a pack of lions toward a river where enormous crocodiles waited for them with big grins.

"Hey, that's not bad," he said admiringly. "They got the dimensions pretty close this time." He pointed. "And see how the mane on the lion is nicely detailed?"

Hedz wasn't into art appreciation.

In a dangerous voice, she growled, "Frigg and Bush. Drew. On. My. Wall."

"Actually, this is my man cave," he said, speaking before his mind could filter out dangerous words. This seemed to happen a lot, so perhaps he had a defective mind-filter.

Silence.

Hedz just looked at him.

The boys seemed to have gone into suspended animation and even the centipede stopped crunching on its meal.

The silence was profound enough he could hear the frantic pounding of his heart which was responding to the crisis by pumping additional blood necessary for feeding muscles in flight.

Finally Hedz spoke.

"I'll pretend I didn't hear that."

Her words released the Dementer spell that had frozen the cave.

Bonk's lungs started up again. "Um, yeah, thanks."

"Anyway, they drew on my wall." An emphasis on the 'my' that this time his brain wisely ignored.

"Oh, yeah, right. They shouldn't do that," he stammered. Then he frowned. "Um, why exactly shouldn't they do that?"

"It doesn't come off."

"Who cares? We live in a cave."

A voice came from behind Bonk. "Yeah, Mom. Who cares?"

Hedz stunned Frigg into silence with the 'Mother-Look' she'd invented the previous week, the same Mother-Look that would benefit future mothers for time immortal. Then she continued, "If we leave it there, some day scientists might think we lived like this."

Bonk blinked. "We do live like this."

"Maybe, but I don't want them to know."

More female logic. Too bad there weren't books on the subject, or any other subject for that matter. Not that he'd have read them, unless they had pictures. But it would have been comforting to know someone was looking into the issue of how women thought.

"What's a scientist?" Frigg and Bush chimed.

"None of your business," Hedz snapped. She turned back to her mate. "Now where's breakfast?"

"Breakfast?"

"Yes, breakfast, you know, three square meals a day."

Bonk blinked. Why would someone eat a square breakfast?

"Oh, breakfast," he said, stalling, suddenly remembering why he had been out. He'd gone to get food, then swung over to the bathroom where he caught up on the daily news scratched onto the walls on a daily basis by his friend Deth. After that he had gone to his work area to tinker with a project he'd been working on. The thought of food had simply slipped his mind.

She crossed her arms. "Yes, breakfast."

Time to be inventive.

"There's, uh, no such thing. We just eat when we're hungry. Regular eating intervals like breakfast, lunch and dinner haven't been invented yet."

He grinned hopefully.

Hedz started tapping her foot. "Okay, funny boy. I'm hungry, the kids are hungry, and ..." She gestured at Baby Eff, attached to her like a barnacle. "... I'm too busy to forage right now. Your entire family is hungry and you're the big, bad hunter. So get something to eat now, or, or…"

She looked around the cave, Eff hanging onto her like a baby Orangutan. Bonk's favorite club was leaning on the wall.

Hedz snatched it.

Bonk didn't know if she was going to break it, or club him with it. Neither seemed like a good thing, so he broke for the mouth of the cave. "I'll get you something! I promise. I'll be right back!"

And he ran out.

Chapter 2

After he was gone, Hedz sighed and turned to the boys, "Frigg?"

Frigg's eyes were back on the rock.

"Bush?"

Bush ignored her, too.

"FRIGG AND BUSH."

This got their attention. "Yeah, Mom," they chimed.

"Would you please go get some gator eggs? I saw a nest out near the big tree in the marsh."

"I thought Dad was going hunting," Frigg moaned.

"Do you want to rely on that?" Hedz asked.

They thought about it. They all knew Bonk was an inept hunter. Tall for a caveman, a fast runner but not all that good about putting food on the rock.

"Um. I am kind of hungry," Frigg said.

"Maybe we could just eat the scorpion," Bush suggested, giving the scorpion a hopeful look. The centipede was guarding the corpse with a threatening air.

Then Frigg remembered his brother had a turtle shell full of grubs. "I vote we wait."

Hedz sighed. "No, Bonk's just going to use this as an excuse to go to the Portsbar and hang with his buddies scratching themselves and drinking fermented grapes."

Frigg wiggled his eyebrows, "Or maybe he'll go to Uters where they got hot babes."

A dark look crossed Hedz's face, "What do you know about that place?"

15

Frigg colored, "Oh, uh … it's right next to the baseball field."

"There's no such thing as baseball," Hedz growled.

"Exactly! Which is probably why I couldn't find the field," Frigg exclaimed. "But while I was looking, I saw guys going in there."

Hedz paused, thinking through that logic. Finally, she just shook her head. "He'd better not go there. Now you two go out and get some eggs. And see if you can round up some lizards and some beetles or something."

They hesitated, perhaps considering some kid-rebellion, but the fierce look on her face squelched those thoughts.

"Let's go," Frigg said to his brother.

Bush paused, a bit in pain, mostly because he was sitting on his private parts, which, since he was nude, weren't particularly private. He shifted, sighed, and took a last longing look at the dead scorpion's death throes. Then he let Frigg pull him to his feet.

Then they tumbled out the door.

A moment later, Bush popped his head back in. "Hey, can we borrow Eff?"

"Why?" Hedz asked.

"We need bait."

Hedz crossed her arms, nearly clobbering Eff. "Not with my baby."

Bush rolled his eyes, "She'll be okay. We're her brothers." He just stopped short of adding 'duh' which probably would have ruined his whole day.

She hesitated, thinking about it.

Bush stopped rolling his eyes, and switched them to pleading mode.

"Oh, okay." Eff was done feeding anyway, so Hedz gently pulled her from her breast, and handed the baby over to her brother.

16

"Thanks."

She shook a finger in his face, "Be careful!"

"Yeah, Mom." Another silent 'duh.'

He grabbed the baby. Then Eff and Bush took off for the river.

Chapter 3

Bonk ambled down the path along the river, keeping a wary eye out for dinosaurs. They had been extinct for millions of years, but you never knew, dinosaurs were notoriously tricky creatures.

There was a rumbling sound behind him, and he looked back, expecting storm clouds. Instead, it was the volcano farting out some gas and stuff. He shrugged. It did that on and off all the time.

He was feeling the sting of his mate's words, Still though, he didn't resent them. She had asked him to bring back food and he'd gotten distracted.

Hedz was a good mate who took care of her little family. He remembered the cold winter right after Eff was born where everything was so locked in ice he couldn't find food. They were starving. After eating all of the lice off each other, he and the boys had fed on Hedz's breast milk. It had weakened her, and Eff complained mightily over short rations, but it had given him the strength to go out into the cold one more time. Fortunately, he had stumbled on the frozen corpse of a deer that had tripped over another deer which had starved and frozen to death. The two deer carcasses had gotten them through the worst of the winter.

So she was a good mate, and, of course, her most excellent mustache was the envy of all his buddies.

He was a bit concerned about the prospects of catching anything because in his haste to escape the cave he'd forgotten his spear and club. He'd have to hope he'd find another dead clumsy deer.

Then he saw a strange stick lying on the ground. It was flat and curved with rounded ends. Curious, he picked it up for closer inspection. He jabbed it experimentally in the air. Nope, it wouldn't work to stab prey and it was too light for a club.

Worthless.

He didn't have any weapons and there weren't any dead critters lying around having voluntarily sacrificed their lives for him, so it obviously wasn't meant to be.

Another failed hunt.

Oh, well, he'd given it the old caveman try.

He decided he might as well go to the Portsbar and commiserate with the guys. They had mates and kids, so they would understand his point of view. Plus, he could drink some of the juice that made him feel funny, fuzzy and forgetful. Then they could talk about how cool it would be when they invented sports. And who knew, maybe some tasty fish had committed suicide by beaching itself.

Happy with his new plan, he flung the curved stick at the river, giving it no further thought.

After about five steps something slammed into the back of his head.

"Aack!"

He whirled around, ready to fight.

Nobody was there.

Then he noticed the strange stick on the ground.

Huh, weird. Hadn't he just thrown it?

He whirled the stick again, and turned to walk.

Five steps later.

"Aack!"

He looked around, ready for a fight.

He was alone.

And the stick was back.

"Huh?"

He threw it again.

This time, he watched the stick's flight as he walked along the path, which meant he didn't see the rock jutting up from the ground.

"Aack!"

He tumbled to the ground, which caused him to totally miss the strange stick's elliptical path through where his head would have been had he not been lying on the ground. He also missed seeing the stick gently thud to the ground under some tall grass.

Bonk got up, rubbed his sore head, and looked around for the stick. It was gone.

Chapter 4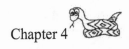

The Portsbar was perched on a cluster of rocks on a sandbar. The sandbar had been formed by a rocky confluence at the mouth of the river feeding into the sea. The saltwater crocs, comfortable in both the river and sea, had an aversion to crawling over the sharp lava rocks, so it was relatively safe. Later in the distant future, the bar would serve as a major port for pirates, and later as the location for a movie about pirates. But now it worked quite well as a drunken hangout for cavemen.

Bonk sloshed through the water. He could see furry outlines on the sandbar. Either his friends or a passing pod of walrus. Walruses didn't mind climbing the rocks and they were ferocious. Since he wasn't armed, he approached with caution.

As he got closer, he could hear voices, which likely ruled out walruses.

(Contrary to later historians, who don't know jack about anything, cavemen had a sophisticated verbal language system. That is, except for a nearby tribe of ferocious little beach dwellers called the Pzones. The Pzones communicated using a complicated system where they held small tablet-sized rocks upon which they tapped arcane messages to each other using just their thumbs. The range sucked, but it would improve in later centuries once G networks and cell towers were invented. Until then they loved it since it allowed them to flaunt their opposable thumbs.)

As Bonk pulled himself onto the rocky ledge, his friend Droog saluted him with a coconut shell full of fermented grape juice. Droog flashed a purple-toothed smile. "Hey, Bonk."

"Dudes," Bonk announced.

(yes, this is the first documented use of the word, 'dude').

A dozen of his friends were in various stages of recline on the rocks. Most waved or grinned except Wug, who frowned and said, "You're late."

Bonk started. "Late? Late for what?"

"For the meeting," Wug said sternly.

"What meeting?" Bonk asked.

"The meeting we are obviously having," Wug growled.

Wug was a tribal elder. Rumor had it he was nearly 'something old.' Nobody knew what that 'something' was because they had no unit of measurement for age. They just knew he'd been there as long as just about anyone, so that qualified him as an elder. As an elder, Wug felt it necessary to convene regular meetings to talk about problems, such as the cave skunk terrorizing the community on a regular basis and the sinking economy, which usually just confused everyone since there was no economy yet or politicians to invent a National Debt.

The cave skunk had been one of the worst troubles. It had proven to be a bit of a prankster, popping into caves and spraying cavemen seemingly just for its own skunkly amusement. They'd finally gotten rid of it by bringing in a cave weasel. Now they were having trouble with the cave weasel.

Wug was hairy and immense, but not immense as in tall. He was wide, really wide, sorta like Sylvester Stallone and Arnold Schwarzenegger strapped together side by side. He took up so much horizontal space he had to slide sideways to get into his cave. The other cavemen used him as a windbreak on hunting expeditions and he once confused a cave bear into thinking he was a rival bear. Hence, his nickname Area Wug.

"Attention everyone. I'm calling this Meeting of Guys to order," Area Wug commanded.

They all looked at him, not so much in respect, but more because there wasn't much going on other than a couple of seagulls fighting over a dead clam on the beach. It was a tossup as to which was more interesting.

"Okay, if you remember, we have a couple items on our agenda. First, we've agreed we're going to start a music group," Wug announced.

Music had been invented inadvertently the week before when a woolly rhino had mistakenly stomped on Wug's foot during a hunt. As a direct result of this incident, Wug had hit the first perfectly pitched E note, and they had found it to be somewhat pleasing to the ear.

"I don't remember anything about a music group," Droog said.

"No, he's right. We did talk about it," Bonk said.

Wug nodded, "Exactly. So let's see if everyone's here." His attention shifted to a small ferrety-looking caveman. "Okay, Berp. Take attendance."

Berp slugged the rest of his drink and belched. Then he looked down at flat smooth rock in his palm. "Okay, role-call, everyone. Here goes, Bonk?"

"Here," Bonk replied.

"Droog?"

"You know I'm here," Droog said sourly. Droog was a notorious grouch, so Berp knew to ignore him and move to the next name.

"Gupp?"

Nobody answered.

Berp looked up. "Is Gupp here?"

"Gupp got eaten by the giant cave weasel last week," Droog said.

"Oh, darn, well, I'll cross his name off the list."

23

"You don't have a list," Droog retorted.

"Yeah, I do, see?" He gestured to the flat rock.

"There's nothing on that rock," Droog pointed out.

Berp shot him a glare, "When I say 'list,' I mean figuratively." He waited to see if there were more objections, and when there weren't he 'ahemed' and continued, "Lunk?"

Nobody answered.

"Lunk? Where's Lunk?"

A group shrug.

"Is Bump here?"

Shrug.

"Dork?"

Another shrug.

"Tork?"

Shrug.

"Yub?"

Shrug.

"Bif?"

"Here," a hairy caveman raised his arm, disturbing a large stench that had taken up residence in that warm area.

"Argh!" everyone downwind cried.

"Oh, sorry about that." Bif lowered his arm. Fortunately, a small salty sea breeze picked that moment to gust the stink away to go find another armpit to take refuge in.

Bonk held his nose. "I move that we come up with a new way to raise our hands without lifting our arms."

"At least until antiperspirant is invented," Droog added.

"Hardy, hair, hair," Berp said.

"Don't you mean, 'Hardy, har, har'?" Bonk asked.

Berp gave him a look. The little caveman was shaped like a penguin, with narrow shoulders, wide hips and a long nose. "No, I mean 'Hardy, hair, hair.'"

"I dunno," Bonk said. "Hardy, har, har sounds way better."

Berp scowled, "Look, I'm one of the first humans ever, and since I'm making up the saying for the first time, I can't be wrong. Even better, everyone from now on will credit the saying to me."

He sniffed. "So make up your own sayings."

The cavemen watched in bemusement.

Berp's scrawny chest was heaving with passion ... no, probably not passion since he was a guy, but definitely something.

He looked down his long nose at Bonk. "You got it?"

"Yup," Bonk said affably, distracted by a small crab that attempted to scuttle by. He picked up and inspected the little creature, watching the legs scrabble in the air. Then Bonk stuffed the crab into a small black bag with white spots. He had gotten the bag when a small skunk – not the prankster skunk - had wandered into their cave one evening. The skunk had been as surprised as they were, and reacted with its typical defense technique. Unfortunately for the skunk, the smell-bomb had smacked into Bonk's family, absorbed the foul stench of the small family of non-bathers and bounced back, stunning the skunk into unconsciousness. Before it could gather its wits, Hedz had clubbed it. Then she had made a bag from the pelt.

Heedless of this story, Berp continued his role call, "Okay, let's see. Deth?"

"Here."

Tacks."

"Here," another caveman answered.

"You can always count on Deth and Tacks," Droog snickered in an aside to Bonk.

"Did I miss anyone?" Berp asked.

"Yeah, you missed me."

Berp looked up. "Oh, Steve, yeah, sorry about that." Steve was white and mostly hairless, a reject from another tribe that was surely doomed to extinction. They had taken him in and

25

pretty much ignored him ever since. Berp pretended to make a note on his note rock and turned around to Area Wug. "Well, not everyone's here, but we have enough for a quorum."

"I don't care about a quorum," Wug said. "As long as we have enough for a band."

"Um, well, I don't know how many people it takes to make a band, but I think we're okay," Berp replied.

Area Wug rubbed his hands together, "Okay, here's what we do. First, we need instruments. Anyone bring any?"

"We have rocks," Droog said.

"Rocks?" Wug said with disappointment in his voice. "Anything else?"

Nothing.

"Okay, rocks it is," Wug replied. "We'll be a rock band."

"If we used mammoth bones would we be a bone band?" Deth wondered.

"Or how about leaves? Or would we have to leave?" Tacks asked.

Area Wug shook his head. "No, we'll use rocks. Mostly because that's all that's on the bar right now."

"I think we're going to look cool, what with our long hair and stuff," Deth gushed.

Everyone looked at him.

He shrugged, "What? We have long hair. Isn't it awesome?"

"The alternative being?" Bonk asked.

"Um, short," Deth said.

"You dork. We can't make our hair short," Wug sneered.

"No, he's not Dork," Berp said, after a quick glance at his list. "Dork didn't make it today."

"That's not what I…" Wug started.

"I call dibs on being the drummer," Tacks announced.

"I think we all have to be drummers," Deth said. "It's not like we have guitars, pianos or anything."

26

Everyone gave him blank looks.

Then Wug said, "Okay, everyone grab rocks."

Some of the cavemen picked up handfuls of small rocks, others had a rock in each hand, and a few grabbed the biggest rocks they could find.

"Now what?" Tacks asked, shakily holding a boulder over his head.

"We make music," Wug said.

"Duh," Berp added.

They all stood, waiting for the music to happen.

"I think we have to do something," Bonk finally said.

"Okay, how about this?" Droog smacked two rocks together.

The flat sound was quickly swallowed up by the low waves lapping against the rock.

"Kind of weak," Wug said.

"Let me try this," Tacks said. He slammed his boulder onto the rocks, spraying shards of splintered rock. The cavemen howled as they were pelted by sharp pellets of stone.

"Music hurts!" Steve yelled.

Wug crawled behind the boulder he'd hidden behind. "Well, I think it's clear music is entirely too painful. I doubt it if will ever catch on."

"Bummer," Deth said, tossing his rocks into the waves.

Bonk dropped his rock, too. "Well guys, it's been a slice, but I was supposed to be hunting."

"Yeah, me, too," Droog said.

The cavemen started climbing over the rocks.

"Hey, I didn't adjourn the meeting," Wug cried to their backs.

"Meeting adjourned," Droog threw over his shoulder.

"Fine," Wug called out. "The top item on the next agenda is God. Don't be late."

27

As Bonk and Droog walked away, Droog whispered out of the corner of his mouth, "What is God?"

Bonk just shrugged.

Chapter 5

As Bonk walked home, a shadow passed overhead, and he looked into the vivid blue sky (politicians hadn't sold air out to industrial polluters, mostly because there weren't any industrial polluters yet).

An enormous eagle was in full dive, its prey a huge flightless bird the cavemen simply called, "Big Bird." Big Bird was much prized by the cavemen for its delicious, huge drumsticks, though the wings - very small vestigial things - were disappointing. This likely delayed invention of the first chicken wings concession, and future Big Birds from obtaining big NBA contracts despite their stellar height.

Big Bird had sighted the eagle and was in full gallop, dodging and weaving through the underbrush. The eagle had short wings for its size and huge tail feathers so it could maneuver through wooded areas and crowded malls, and it simply veered, easily following Big Bird's escape route. Big Bird opened its beak and squawked out a raucous cry of fear, eyes wide with panic. The eagle answered with its own piercing war cry, flexing wicked talons in anticipation of rending flesh.

Big Bird should have paid more attention to the terrain, which went suddenly from terra firma to terra not-so-firma.

It had run right into a tar pit, known by the locals as That Big Stinky Place.

The bird's legs were immediately sucked into the unrelenting muck and the bird's body toppled into the tar with the plopping sound of a fat guy in a mud-wrestling contest. The eagle screeched in triumph and dived with a weighty thump

29

onto Big Bird's back. The eagle's vicious beak started tearing into Big Bird, yanking feathers from its helpless prey. The weight of the heavy birds, combined with their thrashing struggles pushed them deeper into the black tar.

Bonk watched the spectacle with fascination.

"Pretty cool, huh?" someone commented.

"Aaagh!" Bonk yelled, jumping eight and a half inches into the air (this could be determined because he leaped the exact height of a nearby small weed which measured exactly eight and a half inches high.)

When Bonk landed, he whirled to confront the Someone.

He backed off when he saw it was his slightly peculiar friend, Dork.

Dork was a visionary caveman who often spoke of future events with an air of knowledge that the other cavemen couldn't understand. He spent most of one summer trying to get the other cavemen to do something called 'investing' into a fruit. He assured them that Apple would make them wealthy beyond their wildest imaginations and they'd be resistant to viruses and worms. He couldn't explain why investments in Orange and Grape wouldn't yield the same results. Anyway, he was tolerated because he was amusing.

"What are you doing here?" Bonk asked, the bird fracas momentarily forgotten.

"Just studying this oil byproduct," Dork said, indicating the tar pits. Bonk looked just in time to see a methane bubble fart on the oily surface. "Some day people will use it for waterproofing, insulation, even as a low grade fuel and asphalt."

"Oh, okay." Bonk nodded agreeably, while thinking to himself, 'Huh?'

It was usually better not to question Dork about anything for fear he might actually attempt to explain what he was talking about. Which rarely resulted in understanding, so it was better to avoid asking.

Bonk looked back out at the birds, and saw Big Bird mostly engulfed by the tar. The eagle was standing on its back but had somehow gotten its head stuck in the tar. It strained to pull away from the sticky substance and finally, with the sound of pulling a pacifier from a baby's mouth, it managed to retrieve its head from the black surface. The tar kept most of the feathers as a souvenir.

The eagle shook its head, dislodging what few head feathers remained, opened its beak … and croaked. No, it didn't die, but a few nearby frogs perked up in interest. The eagle's beak was gummed up with black muck. Irritated, it shook its head again and then launched into the air.

As the majestic bald eagle soared overhead, Bonk and Dork stood and saluted.

"What are we doing?" Bonk whispered out of the corner of his mouth.

"I don't know," Dork whispered back.

"Oh, well okay, then," Bonk said.

As it turned into a dot in the horizon, Bonk turned to his friend, "Gotta get back. Later."

"Later," the eccentric caveman replied.

Chapter 6

Frigg and Bush slid down the pebbly slope. With Eff slung under his arm, Bush grabbed branches to keep his balance, the baby giggling as she was jostled on the rocky ride.

"You know what?" Frigg asked, sliding like a downhill skier through a particularly slippery patch.

"What?" Bush said, barely feeling rocks gouging into the thick calluses on his feet.

"We need to invent the first cuss word," Frigg responded.

Bush shot his brother a look. Frigg was born the season before Bush and automatically assumed it made him smarter and stronger. Actually, he was, but that kind of thing shouldn't be a given.

"What's a cuss word?" Bush asked.

Frigg grunted, breaking into a jog as they hit the bottom of the hill. "It's a word that makes parents nuts."

Bush frowned. "Like taxes?"

Frigg shook his head. "No, not like that. A cuss is a made up word. You use it to suggest someone should copulate with himself."

"You can't copulate with yourself." Bush paused, considering. "Wait, maybe Tacks could."

Frigg grinned. "True. If anyone could, it would be Tacks. Anyway, you tell them to do it because it's a physical impossibility."

"What's the point of that?"

"You use it as an insult, to make them angry."

"How would that make them angry?"

"You're telling them that they can't get a woman, so they have do it themselves."

Bush thought for a moment, never an easy thing for him. "Okay, why would you want to make them angry? Wouldn't they just beat you up?"

"No, that's the beauty of it. You only cuss when there's no way they can catch you. Or if you're bigger."

"Or if you have them outnumbered?"

"Exactly."

"Oh." Bush still wasn't positive he understood the concept.

Frigg led them down the path leading to the river. Big fat-leafed trees lined the path, dappling the shadows, but the path itself was clear. Above, a thin cloud of smoke rose from the nearby volcano.

As the big yellow thing in the sky shone warmth on his brown, furry back, Frigg thought how good it felt to be naked and alive.

"I think it should start with 'F'," Bush said, keeping an eye on the shadows. It never hurt to keep an eye out both for prey or predators.

"What's that?" Frigg asked.

"The cussword. I think it should be an 'F' word."

"Yeah, okay, good idea. How about 'Jorj'?"

"Jorj'?" Bush's furry eyebrows shot up, making him appear more chimp-like than usual.

"Yeah. So when you get mad at someone, you just say, "Jorj you!"

"Cool," Bush gushed.

"Or if you drop something on your foot, you yell, "Jorj it!"

"Awesome!" Then Bush frowned. "But does 'Jorj' start with an 'F'?"

Frigg shrugged, "I dunno. Nobody invented the alphabet yet. We'll just say it's a French word and the 'F' is silent."

"What's a French?" Bush asked.

"Well, nothing yet, but it will be some day, and then that sentence will make sense."

Bush's face brightened. "Oh, okay. Jorj it is then."

They neared the river which at times was more of a muddy creek, depending on rainfall and drought. When it gorged on massive rains during flooding season, it was a raging, dangerous force. However, the cavemen simply avoided it then, since they never swam or washed themselves and clothes weren't invented and nothing needed to be cleaned. So when it was flooding, the river was essentially a non-factor to the caveman community. For them the river was more dangerous during the non-rainy season when huge ferocious crocodiles moved in from the salty ocean to breed, lay eggs and nest.

They were nesting now, and Frigg and Bush were planning on taking advantage of the seasonal croc invasion.

They dropped onto the river bank, and stood by the river. Upstream was the marshy area where the crocodiles hung out. Downstream led to the sea. Cattails and lily pads gathered wherever the water stilled.

"Now what?" Bush asked.

"We set the bait," Frigg responded. He took Eff from Bush and put the baby carefully on a dry spot on the riverbank. Eff reached out a chubby hand, grabbing sand and shoving it in her mouth. She chewed thoughtfully for a moment, then spit it back out with a look of distaste on her face. She immediately popped another handful into her mouth.

Frigg gathered driftwood, and arranged it as a small barrier to keep the baby from crawling into the river.

"Okay, here's what we do," Frigg said. "The croc is there." He pointed at a small marshy inlet with tall swamp grass. "I'm going to go in and stir up Momma Croc. She'll chase me out, but she won't want to go far from her nest. After she gives up chasing me, she'll see Eff and figure on an easy lunch. That will take her farther from the nest. Meanwhile, you hide behind the nest and when she comes out, it's your turn."

"My turn to what?"

"The eggs. You grab the eggs."

"What about Eff?" Bush asked.

"I'll grab her when I run past," Frigg assured him.

Bush grinned. "Sounds like a plan."

They moved quietly over the sand towards the rush covered nest. They could hear a low growl reverberating from the darkness. Their skin shivered from the vibration of vocalizations too low pitched for caveman ears.

As they got closer, the sand ended and marsh began. Crocs had excellent hearing, but the boys didn't care because the plan was for her to discover them. Frigg motioned Bush to circle around the nest. Meanwhile, Frigg started making more noise to mask the sounds of his brother. The thicket of grass stopped rustling, and there was a loud hiss. Frigg ignored the warning and tromped heavily into the shallows.

He glanced over his shoulder at Eff who was happily sucking on a piece of driftwood. She saw him and gave him a gummy smile around the wood.

That's when the three-ton croc lunged out of the thicket with a tremendous roar.

"JORJ!" Frigg cried, tumbling backwards with a splash.

Huge jaws gaping, the lizard launched at him.

"JORJ!" Frigg shrieked again, scrambling backwards in the water.

On the shore, Eff clapped at the exciting spectacle.

Meanwhile, further up the shoreline, something else roared even louder than the croc, fueling the commotion of many little bodies freaking out all at the same time.

Frigg ignored the other noises, because he had enough on his mind with a hungry crocodile. With its huge webbed feet and powerful lashing tail, the crocodile propelled itself after Frigg.

Startled by the reptile's unexpected speed, Frigg froze.

When it saw its adversary stunned into immobility, the croc raced towards him, eggs momentarily forgotten.

Adrenaline finally unfroze Frigg and he tumbled sideways, rolling awkwardly to his feet.

"JORJ! Bush, hurry up!" he cried.

Bush seized the opportunity and dove headfirst into the nest.

Up the riverbank, the something else that had roared did so again, triggering frenzied movement in the trees. Suddenly dozens of forms erupted from the trees, followed by the huge, lumbering something towering high above the underbrush.

Meanwhile, Frigg had his own problems. Though crocodiles tired quickly, they were capable of incredible speed for short distances. Frigg knew once he made it to shore he could outrun a croc on land. But this crocodile either hadn't gotten the memo, or it was in better shape than its brethren - or in this case, its sisthren. It galloped after him like a ferret on caffeine.

"JORJ!' Frigg shrieked, splashing through the shallow reed-filled muck.

Meanwhile, in the croc's nest, Bush encountered a surprise of his own, "Jorj!" Bush screeched. There weren't any eggs in the nest. Instead, thirty baby crocodiles snapped at him with impressive dentistry.

Back on shore, Eff sensed motion just before small agile hands snatched her up. She shrieked in laughter.

Frigg heard, "Eff!"

Then the croc was on him.

The crocodile's jaws were wide enough to swallow Frigg in a single bite. He juked left, and scrambled up the grassy riverbank. He felt rather than heard the huge creature catapult itself onto the turf.

Meanwhile, Bush dodged the snapping teeth of the baby crocs, deftly grabbing two of the lizards behind the head. Then he jumped out of the nest.

A huge rush of air blasted Frigg as the crocodile thumped onto the ground behind him. He leaped to the side, rolling like a marine. When he reached his feet again, he saw to his horror that Eff wasn't on the riverbank.

Frantically, he looked down the path, and then he saw her. With Meefs.

The Meefs were a small tribe of humanoids who had descended from squirrels. They had fluffy tails and moved with quick little movements. Unlike Bonk's tribe, they weren't carnivorous, preferring instead little nuts that tasted a lot like pizza (a food that hadn't been invented yet).

Why had they taken Eff?

Then he saw what was chasing the Meefs and the question flew from his mind.

Xenarthra. The giant ground sloth.

Five tons of omnivorous fury spread out over twenty-foot of ugliness. Due to its immense size, huge saber-like claws and nasty temperament, the ground sloth feared nothing and was feared by all. Even cave lions gave it a wide berth. Unlike its descendants, it was an indiscriminate omnivore, eating leaves, fish, small animals, anything it could reach. This particular sloth had declared this entire area part of its territory.

"Jorj!" Frigg yelled, breaking out in pursuit.

The crocodile twisted after him, and continued her pursuit.

Eff giggled at the ticklish clever hands holding her. The owner of those hands ran with bursts of erratic speed down the path. Behind them, the sloth crashed through trees, knocking them aside as if they were twigs.

Gripping the baby crocs tightly, Bush chased the mother crocodile ...

... which was chasing his brother ...

... who was chasing a giant ground sloth ...

...that was chasing squirrel-like Meefs ...

...who were running with his sister.

Chapter 7

The bull mastodon idly ripped through the underbrush, casually tearing up small trees with its prehensile trunk. He stuffed the huge salad into his gaping mouth, grinding innocent plants to fiber with huge molars. The mastodon and its herd blithely trampled through the forest, devouring everything green in their path.

A tree dropped to the ground. The mastodon reached down to pick it up and paused as it caught sight of a delectable smelling plant. Even better, buried under the soil beneath its tasty upper growth was a legume it had never before encountered. The mastodon inhaled rapturously, the sweet smell stimulating some part of its brain in a way it had never experienced. This wondrous smell would henceforth beguile the pachyderm species forever.

A peanut.

A mastodon's trunk is so tactile it can pick up a single blade of grass. With this sensitive instrument the mastodon wrapped its trunk around the morsel and with gentleness not normally associated with elephants began to extract it from the soil.

What the mastodon didn't know was something else had already claimed the nut. This animal was a remarkable survivor able to live through anything anywhere on Earth. Its descendents and species would survive many gruesome tortures throughout its plentiful lives on Earth. It would survive cancer testing, and attacks by hawks, snakes, cats, lizards, foxes, weasels, badgers, coyotes, tarantulas and young pre-teen girls, whose attacks generally didn't include eating them.

The mouse.

The ultimate survivor.

In the end, they would outlast even the mighty mastodon and the woolly mammoth.

The whole concept of an elephant being afraid of a mouse was ludicrously ridiculous, even more when the elephant is the ancient mastodon, standing twelve feet tall, weighing twelve tons, with curving ten foot tusks each weighing a ton.

Its adversary, Mus Cornu, the prehistoric horned mouse, topped the scales at maybe twenty grams, less than a mastodon's tooth.

They could hardly be adversaries, right?

But when the giant mastodon wrapped its trunk around the peanut plant, the horned mouse said to itself in effect, 'Wha? That's my peanut!'

There was no way this particular horned mouse was going to let his peanut disappear into the huge maw of a prehistoric elephant. At least, not without a fight.

So the mouse did what any self-respecting rodent would do.

It charged.

Tiny sharp horns stabbed into the sensitive snout of the mastodon. Hurt, surprised and shocked, the mighty pachyderm trumpeted in pain and dropped the peanut. The rest of the herd reacted to the bull elephant's bugling, and the building-sized pachyderms began to nervously lumber away. A mastodon had few predators, but there were a few nasty beasties out there, like saber-toothed tigers and lions. So even mastodons responded when they sensed danger.

And with typical herd mentality, when one mastodon reacted, they all reacted. And with one of their favorite tactics.

Stampede.

40

Pachyderms are known to be among the most intelligent creatures ever. Some scientists believe that they have a sort of collective mind, with memories spanning eons and distances. The memory helps the matriarch elephant lead her herd over miles of desert during draughts, knowing from herd memory where the watering holes are located even when traversing areas she had never before visited.

So as the herd mass trampled down the path, building speed and momentum, the collective mind discussed the situation.

"What happened?" one elephant rumbled.

"A demon got me," the bull replied, his red eyes rolling.

"Whoa!" the other said, pillar-like legs thundering down the path.

"A demon?" another elephant exclaimed.

"What kind of demon?" the first one asked.

"I don't know," the bull cried. "It appeared as a mouse."

"A mouse?" another asked, losing a step in surprise.

"Yes. With fearsome weaponry. They are tricky, hurtful creatures, capable of injuring us, or worse…"

(pause)

"… crawling up our trunks to consume our brains."

"Aaieeee!" the elephants trumpeted, trampling everything in their path.

And the elephant's fear of mice was born.

Chapter 8

Hedz picked up the slobbered-on scorpion. The centipede had feasted until there was nothing left but the exoskeleton. Then the many-legged critter had disappeared into a fissure in the cave wall, leaving Hedz stuck with the disposal of its meal and no tip.

Sighing, she went to the cave entrance and flung the corpse down the slope. She went back into the cave, and noticed Bonk's club. So he wouldn't be bringing home food. Good thing she'd had the foresight to send the kids out, too.

She looked around the cave. Their sleeping pit could use more rushes. The pit was a hollowed out spot on the floor, filled with pebbles covered with grasses and then fur. When the entire family was tucked securely against each other it was a very comfortable place to sleep. The lice seemed to agree, and their own colony was thriving. Hedz didn't really mind the lice, since they were a good source of protein when other food was scarce. She made a note to herself to send Gop to gather more rushes when she got back from her sleepover.

Speaking of Gop, where was the girl?

She went back to the cave entrance to look for her daughter, just in time to see a Meef rush by the path below. Then another, and another, and then another, but this one had something in its clever little hands.

"Eff?" Hedz whispered.

The little baby heard and gave a delighted wave.

"Eff!" Hedz shrieked. She started to run down but then skidded to a stop and rushed back into the cave. She snatched the club and raced back out.

When the Meefs saw the enraged cavewoman storming down the hill in a one-person cavalry charge, they skidded to a stop.

Eff warbled in delight and peed on the creature holding her. She grinned as the wetness spread.

Meanwhile, the crocodile chasing Frigg,

...who was chasing the giant sloth,

...which was chasing the Meefs,

...who were held at bay by a torked-off cavewoman,

... just happened to look over her back to see Bush clutching two of her baby crocs. Enraged, the crocodile let out a throaty roar and spun her enormous body around, thick tail knocking down a small tree. Bush put on the brakes and let out a little pee spurt of surprise. As the great crocodile rushed at him, Bush sprinted back the way he had come.

In the same moment, Frigg picked up a stone and hurled it at the sloth. The rock crashed onto the sloth's back and the monster pirouetted with a speed and grace a sloth was not supposed to have. It reared to its full twenty-foot height and bellowed, the force of its roar and rather nasty halitosis blowing leaves off the trees. The sloth's small red eyes rolled in anger, and it stomped towards Frigg, probably not with the intention of dancing. Frigg wheeled and bolted the other way.

So now Hedz was running after the Meefs,

... who were now following the giant sloth,

...which was pursuing Frigg,

...who was running behind the huge crocodile

... which was chasing Bush,

... who was bolting towards the marsh with his hands full of baby crocodiles.

Then the ground began to vibrate.

Chapter 9

Though descended from squirrels, the Meefs shared several similarities with the cavemen. They were social and tribal, with smaller family groups that were very protective of each other.

Meefs also saw themselves as prey of many creatures, so their sympathies were with other creatures they considered to be prey. They were known to follow predators stalking through the forest, scampering safely above them through the trees calling out warnings and throwing branches and nuts on the predators.

Meefs were also notoriously shy, so shy in fact, scientists have never discovered evidence of their existence. But at one time they were a vibrant and chatty member of the prehistoric community.

The reason they had taken the baby from the riverbank was to protect her from the giant sloth. Hedz had no way of knowing this, and they didn't have time way to communicate it to her, seeing as Hedz's big club didn't invite discussion. And now they were chasing after the sloth, which had previously been pursuing them. Meefs had a great sense of humor and if they hadn't been so frightened they might have found the whole thing wildly ironic.

"What's that?" Cheef the Meef said, as they sprinted.

"What that?" his mate Deef said, whiskers whirring.

"The land is moving," Cheef pointed out, which shouldn't have surprised Deef too much, since the ground was, in fact, shaking, causing them to stumble. Fortunately, Meefs are very

45

agile both on and with their feet. Their toes were nearly prehensile, and they could use them nearly as well as their hands.

"Oh, yeah, that," Deef agreed. "Don't know."

"It's like ground rumble," Cheef said, leaping over a small boulder.

Ground rumble was their word for earthquake, an all too frequent event in this younger Earth.

"No, not that. I see now. I think it be animal mountains." Deef pointed at the herd of upset mastodons lumbering at them, trampling trees, pulverizing ground and startling birds into taking flight. A huge dust cloud shadowed the leviathans as they trumpeted their impending arrival.

"This not be good," Cheef said.

Eff burbled her agreement, and the Meef gave the cave baby's butt a reassuring little pat. When he felt wet, Cheef immediately pulled his hand back, and wished someone would get around to inventing diapers.

Deef nimbly leaped over a small boulder. "Where go we now?"

Cheef quickly glanced behind them. The cave mother was still in pursuit, her mouth moving in what were likely unpleasant words inaudible over the impending stampede. Ahead, the sloth slowed as it finally took notice of the charging mastodons.

The boys and large river reptile were gone, having disappeared down the slope leading to the river. While he didn't care all that much about the croc's safety, Cheef hoped the boys were okay.

"Goes there," Cheef said, pointing up the side of the hill. The sloth was a great climber and could easily follow them up the hill, but the rampaging mastodons couldn't. Still, the mastodons might be enough to distract the sloth.

Deef nodded, and scrambled up the hill, Cheef right behind her. The rest of the tribe scampered behind. A grim and determined cavewoman followed.

They crested the hill and found themselves in a large clearing. There were no trees or cover of any sort. There were, however, a dozen twenty-foot pillars of logs arranged in a large semicircle. Each of the pillars was comprised of several tree trunks lashed together with vine.

The Meefs chirped with delight, and scampered up the pillars.

At the top was a caveman.

He waved. "Hi."

"Eek," The Meefs turned around and ran headfirst down the trunks, claws easily grasping the rough wood. They quickly ran up another pillar.

The tops were flat, connected by logs horizontally lashed to the tops. The semicircle was enormous.

The Meefs squatted, and studied the caveman who grinned at them with yellow teeth. Bits of meat were lodged in his teeth, practically begging for the invention of floss. The vegetarian squirrels weren't encouraged by the meaty smile.

"Welcome to Woodhenge."

"Who you?" Cheep asked, diplomacy not a strong point in Meef society. Neither were lies, stealing or murdering, so it's probably okay to overlook the eventual lapse of manners.

The caveman jabbed a thumb in his chest. "I'm Dork."

The squirrels chattered among themselves.

"What do you here?" Deef asked.

Dork eyed them, lazily scratching himself and displacing a few flies. "Well, I'll be happy to tell you, but maybe you can first tell me what you're doing with that young thing." He pointed at Eff who was busy sucking on the end of a small branch.

"This she?" Cheef said. "Save she from giant claw monster."

"Giant claw monster?" Dork asked.

"Yes," Deef said. She stood and walked across a beam in a passable imitation of the ground sloth's lumbering gait.

Light dawned in Dork's eyes. "Oh, the ground sloth. Yeah, that monster's a menace all right."

Suddenly there was a growl below.

Dork looked down, half expecting to see a saber-tooth tiger. "Oh. Hi, Hedz."

She ignored him, her eyes on the squirrel holding Eff. Hedz was wielding a club nearly as big as herself. Now she reared back to slam it into the pillar.

Cheef's tail fluffed and he looked ready to bolt in any one of several directions.

"Hey! Whoa! Don't break my henge," Dork cried. "Do you know how hard it is to construct these logs without a pulley?" Then he muttered to himself, "I have to invent one of those pretty soon."

Hedz's grip tightened.

"We no take your cub for problem," Deef cried.

"Protect from giant claw monster," Cheef said.

Eff warbled agreement around a mouth full of branch and slobber.

Hedz paused.

Then two more cavemen showed up. Or more precisely, caveman and cave girl. Tacks and Gop.

"Mom, what's going on?" Gop asked.

"Hey, Dork, what's going on?" Tacks asked at the same time.

As Dork and Hedz tried to talk at the same time, Hedz shot him a glare. Dork shut up and let her speak.

48

"These … creatures …" Hedz indicated the squirrel tribe perched overhead who waved timidly, "took Eff and ran up here, to this … I, I .. don't know what it is."

"Woodhenge," Tacks and Dork said together.

"Okay, Woodhenge. They took her. My baby." A dark look went over her face. "So I'm going to skin myself some squirrels and get my baby back."

"NONONONONO," the Meefs cried.

"I don't think they meant any harm," Dork said. "They took her to keep her safe from the ground sloth."

"Maybe, maybe not," Hedz growled.

"They don't eat meat," Dork said. "I think she's perfectly safe."

Hedz looked up at the Meefs. The squirrel humans had black furry hands with opposable thumbs, small ears close to their head, and liquid eyes. The Meefs looked back, nodding and smiling rodent smiles, their big chewing teeth white and shining like a Chiclets commercial.

"Okay," Hedz said, somewhat convinced. She dropped the club. "So give me my baby."

"Kay-oke," Cheef said.

With a slurping sound, he gently broke Eff's mouth's seal on the branch and claws digging deeply into the wood he brought her down the side of the log. Prudently keeping out of Hedz's reach, he handed the baby over. Eff giggled as fingers tickled her.

Hedz took Eff, and with eyes bright with tears hugged her ferociously.

Crisis averted, Eff's sister Gop looked around at the henge. "So what's this thing?"

"I'm making a wood henge," Dork said proudly.

"And I'm helping," Tacks said, eyes shining deep under jutting supraorbital ridges. "Me and Deth."

Gop looked around. "Deth? I don't see Deth anywhere."

49

Tacks grinned, "Oh, he's not here now. He's out killing something."

"So what exactly is Woodhenge?" Gop asked.

Dork's eyes lit up. He was always ready to explain stuff to enlightened cavemen, especially since it was hard to find enlightened cavemen. "A henge is a meeting area that will be used for governmental meetings and religious ceremonies."

"What's religion?" Gop asked.

"What's governmental?" Hedz asked at the same time.

Dork ignored this and jabbed a hairy finger into the air. "And it will be a great place to escape flooding."

"Because it's so high in the air," Tacks put in.

Gop looked around doubtfully. "But you're already on a hill."

"And you made it out of wood," Hedz added. "If a flood hit here it would just float away."

Dork thought on that point, and his face fell. "That's right. I never thought of that."

He frowned, and mumbled to himself, "I may have to use stone." He looked down at his helper. "Tacks, get up here."

"Okay," Tacks said agreeably and looked for a handhold. There was a branch just out of his reach. He looked at the two cave females. Hedz's hands were full of baby. Gop was good-sized, for a female. "Hey, Gop, give me a hand here, okay?"

Gop shook her head, "Nope, sorry, no matter what I won't raise Tacks.

Chapter 10

At the bottom of the hill the giant sloth braced as the mastodons rushed by, urgently trumpeting their fear of mice running up their trunks. As they whooshed by, the sloth swung a meaty punch at them, huge claws slicing through air. With more agility than one might expect, the pachyderms neatly avoided the claws and disappeared down the path with ground-jarring haste.

As they faded out of sight and sound, the sloth was left alone. The Meefs had disappeared. The cave boys were gone. The crocodile was gone.

It was silent.

Except down by the river.

Chapter 11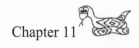

"Aagh!" Bush cried, feeling the force of the massive saltwater crocodile thumping behind him. The big lizard was uncomfortably close and Bush was trying to keep his footing while juggling the snapping baby crocs. His grip on their scaly heads was weakening and he knew he couldn't hold them much longer.

He risked a glance behind him and immediately wished he hadn't. The momma crocodile was on all fours, high off the ground, galloping with a speed he didn't know crocodiles possessed, with an endurance he also didn't know they possessed. Her bulbous eyes were red and glaring.

Behind her, Frigg's eyes were darting, looking for anything he could use to fight the reptile. Finally, he saw something circling overhead.

An enormous eagle.

"Bush! Throw the babies into the water."

"What?" Bush was fully in run-mode, not listen-mode and could barely hear over the crocodile's grunting and the sound of his own wildly beating heart.

"The baby crocodiles," Frigg yelled again, cupping his hands.

"What about them?" Bush cried.

"Throw them in the river!"

"Oh," Bush bolted down the bluff overlooking the river. Sprinting the last few yards, he skidded to a stop, using his momentum to fling one and then the other baby croc into the swift current. The babies hit the water, their thrashing drawing immediate attention from above. A huge shadow passed overhead.

The croc saw the eagle and launched the last ten yards into the water, tons of angry lizard displacing gallons of water in a spectacular splash.

The eagle was in full dive, talons spread wide to snatch the small lizards. The babies were swimming towards the far shore, unaware of the danger screaming in on them like an F16 fighter jet. The same couldn't be said for the mother crocodile, whose thick, lashing tail propelled her rapidly through the water, her large wake mute testimony to her ferocious speed.

The babies reached the far side just as the eagle latched onto the lumpy back of one of the small reptiles, talons ripping through thick skin. The baby arched its back trying to bite at whatever was on its back.

With powerful sweeps of its stubby wings, the eagle lurched skyward, its prey snapping at air.

Digging her thick front claws into a log that had gotten snared in the shallows of the river, the leviathan croc launched her entire upper body airborne, gaping jaws reaching fifteen feet above the ground. She chomped at the eagle which was struggling with its burden.

And missed.

Fortunately her momentum was enough that her gargantuan head butted into the eagle's butt, sending it into a feathery spiral. The baby crocodile thrashed loose and together the big and little crocodiles fell to earth, hitting the mud with a massive thud and a much less massive thwip.

The stunned eagle smacked into the birch while somehow staying airborne. Flapping awkwardly to a high branch in the birch, the bird of prey looked below at its lost meal. Its screech of frustration pierced the air as the second baby crocodile climbed the muddy bank to safety next to its mother. With a last cry of anger, the eagle launched from the branch.

"That eagle has a funny looking head," Bush said.

Frigg nodded, "Yeah, it's like it's bald."

As it flew over the two cave boys, they jerked to attention and saluted.

"Why are we doing this?" Bush asked.

"I don't know," Frigg answered.

They continued saluting until the bird became a dot, and then lowered their arms.

"We gotta go get Eff," Frigg said, his voice catching.

Bush turned white, "Ah, I forgot about her. Let's go."

They turned around, and nearly ran into Gop and Hedz.

When they saw Hedz was holding their baby sister, the boys' faces split into stupid grins of relief.

Hedz wasn't grinning.

Gop was mirroring her mother's glare.

Hedz crossed her arms.

Gop crossed her arms.

"You were supposed to watch your sister," Hedz said, nearly sheering off a molar.

"Um, we, er, .." Bush stammered.

"We, the croc, but a sloth…" Frigg stuttered, his arms waving.

"Tell me you at least got the eggs," Hedz asked, arching a furry eyebrow that cried out for plucking.

"The eggs? But they weren't …" Bush stammered.

"And an eagle…" Frigg stuttered, his arms waving.

"Never mind, come on boys." Hedz whirled and headed back to the cave. Gop followed, perfectly mimicking her mother's posture of immense disappointment.

When they hit the path, there was no sign of the sloth or mastodons. The trail was beaten down, grass pulverized and leaves tattered from the mastodon stampede.

There was a person standing in the middle of the trail.

"Uh, hi, honey," Bonk said.

He pulled open the skunk bag. "Look, honey, I got us breakfast." He took out the tiny hermit crab he'd picked up from the rocks at the Portsbar. Then he flashed a weak grin.

Chapter 12

A few minutes later, a disconsolate Bonk headed towards a new business that had been established by his friend, Joz. A fearless would-be entrepreneur, Joz was making another attempt to establish the very first business establishment. His first attempt was something he called a Swim and Tennis Club. That had consisted of four cavemen standing in a foot of water in the river swinging clubs at birds feeding on mosquitoes. The game ended on a tragic note when a salt water crocodile tried to join in.

His most recent attempt was called Takobehl serving something he called 'fast food.' The food was indeed fast, both in preparation and how quickly it moved through the intestines. Bonk and Hedz used it only as a last resort when neither hunting nor gathering were successful.

"Hey, Bonk," Joz was sitting behind a flat rock, mixing something brownish in a large nut shell. Joz was fiercely protective of the secret ingredients in the glop he served. Bonk figured he was better off not knowing. He was also fairly certain that what Joz called 'meat' wasn't really meat or even a close relative.

"You wants some takos?" Joz asked.

"Yeah, gimme ten," Bonk said, wondering what a ten was as he said it.

"You got it, chief," Joz said.

He reached two dirty fingers into the congealed brown gunk and dropped a blob onto a leaf. Then he folded the leaf over the gunk.

Bonk's nose gave a thumbs up to the smell, but his stomach and intestines rumbled throaty disapproval, perhaps realizing they would soon be rushing the noxious concoction through his system where it would depart his body in mostly liquid form supported by a gaseous cloud capable of burning one's nose hairs.

Yeah, gross.

When Joz was done making the takos, he wrapped them in a bigger leaf and put it on the rock countertop. "Give me some cups please," Joz said, who liked payment in rare utensils.

Bonk obediently handed over three small cups Hedz had fashioned from gourds. Joz rubbed a greasy thumb over them, and content with their quality, handed the takos to Bonk.

"Thanks for coming," Joz said with a greasy smile.

Bonk paused. "You know you're spelling tako wrong, don't you?"

"Huh?"

"Never mind." Bonk headed back to the cave, happily munching his tako.

....

Halfway home, Bonk's body reacted with an urgent need to rid itself of the hastily consumed tako. Bonk sped up, his stomach cramping painfully. At the same time, thunder rumbled from the other side of the hill.

Bonk moved as quickly as his tortured innards would allow towards the small volcanic hole where he and his family evacuated waste. A couple of long rocks overshadowed the fissure, providing protection from the elements and a bit of privacy. A huge seed shell covered the hole. The seed shell cover was born of necessity after a centipede once had crawled out of the hole while Hedz was in residence. Her scream had started a small rockslide that had inadvertently wiped out a family of cave gophers.

Bonk scuttled up to the hole, lifted the seed out of the way and settled in, his eyes on the darkening skies.

A crack of thunder boomed over the small valley, scaring the crap out of Bonk. Fortunately, Bonk was in a convenient place for this, so he quickly wiped with a leaf.

Then the downpour hit and water rushed from the skies, the wind whipping the trees into a frenzied dance. Bonk backed further into the small enclave as lighting strobed the valley with white fury. Thunder boomed overhead and static electricity toyed with his hair.

Then there was a big flash of light, a tremendous boom and a sharp cracking sound echoed from the river amid the torrential rain.

Then, as if turned off by a spigot, the rain stopped.

Bonk peered out from the protection of the rocks into the green gloom. Rain splattered onto the mud and the winds settled into a fresh breeze.

Tentatively, the caveman ventured out onto the path.

He looked up at the sky, and then habitually looked around for danger.

And a light caught his attention.

The old dead tree near the river was crackling and roaring, bathed in yellow and red.

As he approached the tree, heat hotter than the hottest he'd ever felt raged at him, making his eyes smart.

It was fearsome, but exciting at the same time. Something made him want to come closer.

Keeping under the heat, he crept closer until he reached a small bush far beneath the inferno engulfing the top of the tree. A small flame was dancing on the end of a branch.

What was it?

Poking was Bonk's usual method of learning. He had tried the same technique when courting Hedz and it resulted in four kids. So it had its good points and its bad points.

And remember, this is the age before instruction manuals, an invention created for guys to ignore while screwing up something that could have been avoided if said guys would have actually read the instructions.

So he poked the merry flame.

"OW!"

After shaking off the pain and with a bit of trial and error, mostly painful error, he was able to coach the hot stuff onto a branch. Beaming with pride and nursing his wounded hand, he walked across the path to take it home and show Hedz.

A dire wolf and its mate showed up on the path the same time. Huge and shaggy, a dire wolf was larger and meaner than a gray wolf and they weren't adverse to the occasional caveman snack.

"Aghh!" Bonk cried.

"Grrr," the wolves replied, licking their lips, anticipating caveman tasting. And there was nearby water, so they could rinse the stink off first. They circled Bonk, waiting for him to run. Wolves preferred to catch their prey in chase, both for the sport and because it was easier to hamstring a fleeing prey.

Bonk threw a tako at the wolves. The larger one quickly snapped it up, munched wolfily, and horked it back up. It knew real food. It growled again, and took a step towards Bonk. The other wolf snarled and crouched to spring.

Terrified, Bonk brandished the flaming branch at them, like a Pittsburg Steelers fan with a 'Terrible Towel'. Oxygen fed the flames and the fire whooshed.

The wolves backed away uncertainly. This gave Bonk more courage, and he waved the branch at their yellow eyes. He was crazy with fear, yelling horrible battle cries.

"I hope you get cavities because you don't brush!"

"Never swim on a full stomach!"

This confused both the wolves and Bonk.

But while they hesitated, and mustering bravery he didn't know he possessed, Bonk rushed them, screaming and thrusting the flame in their furry faces. The smaller wolf lost her nerve, wheeled and fled. The big male paused, and followed after his pack mate.

Bonk watched them lope away, and as they disappeared into the brush, he grinned widely.

"Yeah! Who's the man? Me! I'm the Man. Master of Fire. Lord of the Flame."

He strutted down the path, brandishing the torch overhead. Then a flaming leaf dropped onto Bonk's hirsute back. Hair singed as flame caught quickly on greasy unwashed back hairs.

"Aaagh!" He tried slapping the flames that leaped greedily from one back hair to the next, painfully toasting skin along the way. Though there was a river nearby, it wouldn't occur to him to jump in to douse the flames.

Then the fire caught onto his long mane of hair. It poofed into a blazing torch.

Aaagh!" he cried, his hair a pyrotechnic-glory that would be repeated at a much later point of time by a pop star named Michael Jackson. Bonk tried slapping the flames, but they were too hot and he tripped around like a river dancer on some kind of hallucinogen. Fortunately, his innate clumsiness handled the problem as he tripped over a rock, slammed onto the ground, and rolled several feet through the sand.

He lay prostate, nose in the sand, feeling sorry for himself and sucking sand into his cranial passages. Coughing violently, the Master of Fire and Lord of Flame made his way back to his feet.

The branch had fallen. It still had flame on one end, so he gingerly picked up the other end, scooped up the remaining takos that had spilled onto the path, and made his way up the hill to the cave. As he climbed, he tenderly felt his crispy hair.

Chapter 13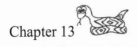

Hedz and Gop were waiting near the cave entrance when Frigg and Bush climbed up the hill, their arms full of rushes.

"Some of these are wet," Frigg said, dumping the rushes on the ground. Bush added his to the pile. Leaving the rushes for the womenfolk, the two boys zoomed into the cave to see if anything was on the rock.

Gop squatted and felt the rushes. "These aren't bad," she said critically.

"Better than sleeping on rock," Hedz said.

She pulled the wet rushes out of the pile, laying them flat to dry. The sun had come out of hiding after the brief but feisty thunderstorm and it was getting muggy. Hedz and Gop shook the dry rushes to loosen any critters and then laid them in another pile while the wet ones dried.

"What's this?" Gop said, pulling something from the rushes.

Hedz looked over and saw another kind of plant mixed in with the rushes. It had a long stem, wavy purple-streaked leaves and a profusion of delicate white flowers. Roots sprouted from a large brown bulb.

"Hmmm," Hedz said, picking up one of the plants.

Bulbs were always a potential food source but could not be served until first tested on cave rats. If the rats ate them, they were safe enough.

She snapped off the bulbs and dropped them in a puddle to rinse. But when she started washing the mud off, something strange happened. The bulbs started lathering, bubbling up on her hands and arms. She tried to wipe the foam off and then something stranger happened. The mud, blood and scabs on her hands loosened. Bemused, she rinsed her hand in the water puddle and the dirt and lather just went away. She sniffed her hand. Not bad. Way better than it had been. And her hand was cleaner than at any time in her entire life.

She decided she liked it.

Gop was watching with a look of fascination and then she duplicated Hedz's experiment, cleaning up to her elbow. She stared with wonder at the expanse of brown skin.

Then Bonk showed up, too excited to notice the unfamiliar cleanliness of his womenfolk. "Look!" he said. He whooshed the flame, careful to keep it away from his back hair.

Hedz and Gop backed up hastily.

"What are you doing with that?" Hedz cried.

"I'm the Fire God!" Bonk declared.

"What's fire?" Gop said, shielding her face.

"This." Bonk thrust the branch at them and they backed against the rock wall.

"Get that away!" Hedz cried.

Bonk's face fell. "But it is a most excellent predator-repellant. I chased away two wolves with it."

That got his mate's interest, "Really? It scared wolves?"

"Yep," Bonk said proudly. "They ran away like a, um, like a…"

"You?" Hedz grinned. She was feeling a bit braver about the yellow flickering flames which seemed inclined to stay on the branch.

"Well, yeah, like me. But that's not really fair," Bonk said defensively. "We haven't invented much in the way of weapons yet, so it's not like I can take on wolves normally."

"So what does it do?" Gop asked, gesturing at the fire.

Bonk looked at the flame. What could they use it for?

"Well, it, uh, um…it's hot."

Gop frowned. "Hot?"

"Yeah, you know, like when the sun makes sand so it hurts to walk on it."

"Which son?" Gop asked, looking back in the cave where Frigg and Bush had disappeared.

Bonk gestured skyward with agitation. "The sun! You know, the flat disk that travels across the sky every day."

Gop blinked into the sun. "Oh, the sky disk. Yeah, it is the same color. Did the fire break off the sky disk?"

Bonk paused. The fire came when the rain fell from the sky, but who was to say it wasn't part of the sky disk? The disk was hiding when the storm started. Maybe it had broken into pieces. Or maybe the rain knocked off a piece of the sky disk.

"What happened to your hair?" Hedz asked, gesturing to the wisp of black smoke drifting from Bonk's head.

He felt the singed hair and grinned sheepishly. "Oh, that, heh, heh."

She squinted critically, "I guess you finally found a way to cut it."

He blinked. "Um, yeah. I did it on purpose. Yep. I did. It worked okay but I still think there's got to be a better way." He looked back up at the flames. "Still, this stuff is pretty cool, huh?"

A burning ember fell from the branch onto the dry pile of rushes.

Whoosh!

"Aagh!" Bonk yelped, jumping backwards.

"My rushes," Hedz cried. She ran towards the fire, but had to back away as flames leaped eagerly upward.

In dismay she watched the flame greedily consume the plants.

Bonk's mouth was open. "It grows," he said in wonder. "It eats hair, it eats plants. What else does it eat?"

He threw a rock into the flames, watching carefully. The rock just sat there, not burning. He looked up to point this out to Hedz, but stopped when he noticed she was glaring at him.

"What?"

Hedz's hands were on her hips, "Nice going, Mr. Fire God. You burned our bedding."

Bonk looked at the raging flames.

"But, but…"

"Yes, I know there will probably be great use for this … fire," she gestured towards the happy flame. "But you have to be able to take care of your toys."

"But, but…"

"So go do something with it," she said.

She disappeared into the cave.

Gop gave a ladylike sniff, and then mimicked her mother, following her inside, leaving Bonk with his flame.

For just a moment, because Hedz came back out and without a word snatched the takos. Then she disappeared back into the cave.

Bonk was left alone with his flame, flames actually. Now he had two, the one in the branch and the one on the rushes.

"I don't care what she says. You're cool," he whispered to the flame, resisting the urge to pet it. Following Hedz's command, he climbed the hill above the cave, swinging the branch and wishing something would come by so he could flame it.

As he went up the hill, he touched the flame to various objects to see what would happen.

Weed, yes. A brief flame and then it crumpled.

A spider's web disappeared without a flash.

Its occupant curled up and turned black.

Rock, nope.

Sand, no.

Lizard, don't know. It ran away before he could touch the flame to it.

He crested the hill, and entered a clearing with enormous log pillars around a semi-circle.

"Whoa. What's this?"

He walked up to one of the pillars. "This is really cool. Wonder if it burns." He touched the branch to the bark. Though damp from the rain, it was dry enough to take the flame.

Bonk backed away as yellow flickered through the logs, slowly fighting for grip. After a moment, he got bored and tried burning some grass.

Nice.

A beetle crumpled in agony, dying a twitching death.

Then Bonk saw a water puddle.

"I wonder if water can catch fire."

He plunged the flame into the puddle and it died in a hissing fit.

Bonk gasped

He yanked the branch out of the water. The fire was gone.

"Noooo!" he howled.

"Noooo!" someone else howled from behind him.

Bonk whirled in surprise.

Dork was batting the flames engulfing the side of the log pillars.

"My henge," he moaned.

"My fire," Bonk cried.

The flames climbed, taking on energy from the sap running down the sides of the logs, drying the damp wood and then burning it as it climbed.

Dork yelped as the flame singed his hand, and gave up trying to put it out. The searing heat drove the two cavemen away, and they watched the flame with fascination, horror and excitement.

Then Bonk noticed something on top of the logs. He pointed. "Look."

An opossum was climbing along the top of the horizontal log, moving at warp-opossum speed as tongues of flame danced along under the log. By the time the opossum reached the other column, the fire was already burning the second column. The opossum peered frantically over the edge and saw only flames. Behind it the horizontal bridge was a roaring mass of flames. There was nowhere for the opossum to go.

So it did what opossums do.

"Look, it died," Bonk cried.

Dork shook his head. "No, it's just pretending."

As the heat got closer to the opossum, it did something it wouldn't normally do.

It peeked.

And saw flames.

Abandoning its acting job, the opossum scrambled around looking for an escape route, the fire raging around it with white heat. Suddenly, the henge flared to a torch and the opossum was engulfed by a furnace. It screeched once.

Dork lowered his head. "I don't think it's pretending anymore."

The cavemen were used to death, which visited their tiny community on a regular basis, taking adults, children, animals. So their hearts did not quail at the tiny creature's death. Instead, the sight of the flames captivated them as fire would on humans for ages.

Then with the suddenness of a Stephen King movie monster, a blackened object fell out of the flame and landed with a thud at their feet. Bonk and Dork screamed. They stopped screaming when they noticed the object wasn't moving.

As Bonk looked at the smoldering mass sizzling in the sand, an aroma hit him and his mouth started watering.

"Do you smell that?"

Dork lifted his chin and took a noisy sniff.

"Wow. That smells really good."

Bonk looked around, "Where's it coming from?"

Dork kneeled next to the cooling hunk of flesh in front of them. "I think it's this."

"The opossum?" Bonk asked. He'd eaten opossum before. It wasn't his favorite food, but until they invented supermarkets they couldn't afford to be too choosy about what they ate.

Bonk stuck his nose next to the dead opossum.

Perhaps he'd underestimated this animal. The savory smell was delectable. His stomach growled, proving it had recovered from the takos, and he was suddenly famished. Hesitantly, he touched the dead opossum. Its flesh was hot, but not too hot for callused caveman fingers. He grabbed the creature's front leg and tugged gently. It pulled away from the body with a tidy snick. He sniffed the meat. It smelled of warmth and something else. Something delicious.

He took a bite, and chewed thoughtfully, enjoying the texture, the warmth. Dork watched with the intentness of a dog at the dinner table.

"Well?"

Bonk chewed a bit more, and swallowed. "This is awesome. You should try it."

Dork didn't need a written invitation. Good thing, considering written invitations wouldn't come around for a few millennia or so.

He grabbed an opossum drumstick, twisted it off, and jammed most of it in his mouth. After a few tentative chews while the new sensations registered, he started masticating with gusto. "Tchis iz gude," he said through a mouthful of opossum.

Bonk tore into another bite, deciding he really, really liked what fire did to meat.

Then he grabbed the rest of the opossum corpse, and raced over the ridge. "Hedz has to try this!"

Behind him, Dork chewed slowly while looking mournfully at his burning henge. He took another bite of opossum, and decided overall, the discovery had been worth it. Then he followed his friend down the hill.

Chapter 14

That night, Bonk and Hedz were sitting at the mouth of the cave, staring into the fire. The kids were inside, resting off full bellies. They'd caught and toasted a gopher, a mole, a vole and a small bird. The only thing missing was ice-cold Coke, which, alas, wouldn't be possible for quite awhile.

The mates snuggled, their fronts toasted by the warm flame. Bonk looked up at bright stars shining in familiar formations in the clean black expanse of sky. He pointed at a particularly bright one. "I hereby name you 'twinkle.'"

"You can't name a light speck," Hedz said sleepily.

"Why not?"

Hedz frowned. "I don't know. It just doesn't seem right."

Bonk just grinned, and pointed at another one. "And that one is named 'Hedz.'

Hedz's eyes widened. "You can't name one after me!"

"Sure I can," Bonk said. "Who's going to stop me? I am the Fire God."

Hedz giggled, and edged closer to her mate.

They sat in companionable silence for a few moments, Bonk's eyes on the star he had just named. "Do you want it?"

Hedz looked at him with drowsy eyes. "What?"

He pointed at the star. "Your light speck."

She squinted up, "I don't know. I guess…"

Bonk leaped up, his eyes on the stars above. He grabbed a stick and poked into the air. "Hmm, I think I need something longer."

He went into a nearby copse of trees and found a young sapling. With casual caveman strength, he snapped off the small tree, scraped off some branches and broke the top so it came to a point. Then he went back to the clearing where Hedz was sitting. Bonk looked back into the sky and found the star Hedz. He jabbed the spear into the sky.

"Whoa, that's farther up than I thought."

"Oh, Bonk, it's not important. Just leave it alone and come sit back down."

"No, I can do this." Bonk studied the star. It seemed so close. "What do you suppose it is? I'll bet it's an ice crystal or something."

He threw the spear into the air. It reached its zenith quite a bit short of its target, and clattered back on the rocks.

"I bet I can reach it from up a tree."

"No, Bonk, don't."

He turned and flashed a smile that had never seen Colgate. "Don't worry. Nothing's too much for Hedz-Bonk-mate."

Turning, he went back to the trees, pausing to pick up his spear on the way.

That's when Hedz saw a black shape flit through the shadows ahead of him.

"Bonk!"

He turned around and grinned. "What, didja miss me already?"

"No, Bonk! There's something there!"

Bonk turned, just as the black shape sprang from the shadows with a deep-throated snarl. Another erupted from the trees.

Saber-tooth tigers.

"Aargh!"

Bonk knew running was the exact wrong thing to do. Instead, he crouched, and growled a warning of his own. Futile perhaps, a bit thready, yeah, because he was scared out of the

71

pants he wasn't wearing. Still, it was a pretty good growl considering.

"I'm coming," Hedz cried.

"No! Get in the cave" His eyes were on the felines bounding towards him.

She ignored him, and he could hear her feet slapping on the ground. He couldn't afford to turn and try to get her to retreat. But now that she was in danger, he felt a new resolve take over, and he growled again, this time with more feeling.

The tigers didn't care. They ignored his warning, and came at him with great bounding leaps.

Bonk's fingers tightened on his spear, and he wished he had a better weapon. A cannon, grenade, laser gun, squirt gun, smelly diaper. Anything more than a slender pole with a point on the end.

Suddenly Hedz rushed by wielding a huge branch with flame.

The tigers skidded to a stop, and snarled. They weren't built like cats. They looked like hyenas on steroids, with long front legs, shorter back legs and thick, muscular bear-like shoulders.

Hedz swung the flaming branch at the tigers and screamed an incoherent battle-cry (it sounded a lot like, 'oh say can you see, by the dawn's early light,' but that couldn't be right.).

One of the tigers tried a flanking move but Hedz swung the branch at the tiger with a huge fiery whoosh. The tiger roared and leaped back. The other tiger tried circling the opposite direction. Hedz cut it off with the flaming branch. Snarling, the cat backed away. Bonk picked up a heavy rock, and with a grunt shot-putted it at the tawny beast. The rock thudded into its muscular side, and the saber-tooth hissed, brandishing eleven-inch incisors.

The cats backed away and that's when two dire wolves showed up, their yellow eyes on the cats.

Two dogs. Two cats. You know what comes next, right? Except one minor detail.

The wolves were about half the size of the saber-tooths.

The cats and wolves sized each other up, the wolves' mouths open in canine grins. Then the cats displayed their huge incisors and the wolves weren't grinning anymore ... mostly because they were running.

The tigers burst into chase after a prey that didn't brandish fire or throw rocks.

As the four predators disappeared into the darkness, Bonk and Hedz exchanged looks. Then they gazed in wonder at the flaming branch.

"We should be dead," Hedz said in a shaky voice.

"This stuff comes in pretty handy. And not only does it work for defense, but it cooks food and burns off unwanted back hair," Bonk said.

Hedz looked around uneasily. "Yeah, maybe, but I think we should get back to the cave."

When they got back to the cave she dropped the smoldering branch onto the pile of ashes which was all that remained of their fire.

"It's getting smaller," she said, looking critically at the embers.

"How do we keep it?" Bonk asked, his status of Fire God at risk

"I don't know," Hedz replied. "I'd like to keep it. It's useful."

"I know how," Bonk said. He grabbed the still damp rushes and dumped them on the fire.

To his horror, the fire disappeared into black billowing smoke.

"Arghh!"

He frantically pulled the rushes from the flame, coughing into the smoke. Finally, overwhelmed by fumes, he staggered backwards and blinked through tears at the smoky ruin that had been his fabulous fire.

"Noooo!"

"I don't think your fire likes water," Hedz said after a moment's reflection.

Bonk groaned.

He should have realized wet was bad for flames since the puddle had put out his earlier fire. He decided not to mention this to his mate.

"We'll just have to get some more," Hedz said.

Chapter 15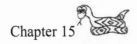

The next morning, Bonk was on the hill, chipping at a rock with a small hunk of granite. He closed his eyes against the spray of rocklets pinging off his face.

After a bit, he cracked the rock one last time, and looked critically at the results. The rock was flat and round and roughly five feet across and a foot deep. Just the way he had planned it.

He gave a grin of triumph. "Hah! Done."

Grunting, the sturdy caveman strained to lift the rock. With a hollow thunk, the rock tipped onto its edge. Then he gave an experimental shove, and after a moment of stubbornness, the rock obediently rolled a couple inches. It had taken relatively little effort. Well, relative to a caveman.

He pushed harder and as the rock rolled he kept pushing and it became easier to move.

Bonk was delighted. "I gotta show everyone."

...

A short while later he was rolling his invention along the path when he came across another caveman named Grog. He wouldn't have been Bonk's first choice to show his new invention to, but Bonk was so excited even Grog would do.

As Bonk tried to stop, the heavy wheel kept rolling, smushing the other caveman's foot.

"Ow, ow, ow!" Grog yelped, jumping up and down. When the pain receded, he looked at the rock with interest. "Hey, what's that?"

Bonk wasn't sure he liked the look in the other caveman's eyes. "I call it a 'wheel.'"

Grog's look was almost predatory. "Really? Can I buy it off you?"

Bonk blinked. He hadn't considered selling it. It had taken a lot of time and effort to build.

Grog gave a cheesy smile, "I promise I'll make it worth your while."

Bonk looked down at the wheel, and then back at Grog. "Well, I guess…"

"Awesome," Grog said. He whipped out a leaf and scribbled on it with a bit of coal. A fortuitous by-product from the burned down Woodhenge. Groml, the first attorney, was still fighting for the copyright.

Grog handed the leaf to Bonk who frowned. "What's this?"

Grog gave a shark grin, "It's a check."

"A check?"

"Yep. A check is a negotiable instrument backed by funds deposited at the bank."

"Bank?" This was over Bonk's head. Did it have something to do with the nearby riverbank? He trusted the river. Maybe not the crocs inside, but the river was another thing. After thirst had been invented, the river had proven to be a valuable and reliable natural resource that should stay clean, at least until the creation of BP Amoco. He scratched under his arm, releasing a foul stench, and he thought it might be nice if someone invented bathing in the near future.

"Yeah. Look, it won't bounce." Grog dropped the leaf on the ground. He was right, it didn't bounce. "See, the check's good. I'll just take my new wheel now." Grog took the wheel, and carefully rolled it away.

As Grog and his wheel disappeared around a rocky outcropping, Bonk looked at the scribbled marks on the leaf, wondering just how to get money out of it. Whatever money was, for that matter.

After a moment, he sighed, and clutching the check in a hirsute hand, strolled over to the riverbank, keeping a wary eye out for crocs. He looked into the river's crystal clear depths. It was still clean and fresh since pollution had not yet been invented or lobbyists giving buckets of money to politicians to protect industrial polluters. After a moment's reflection, he dropped the check onto the river's bank. As the check hit the sand, a gust of wind caught it and it bounced out of sight fluttering manically.

Bonk watched dolefully until it disappeared.

Then he sighed, and headed home towards his cave. He followed the thin line of smoke put out by the volcano, studiously ignoring the tracks from where he had wheeled his wheel down the road earlier.

As he climbed the hill to the cave, he found himself feeling out of sorts, a bit scammed about the whole thing. A check? Negotiable instrument? Heck, they hadn't even invented instruments, so how could they have ones that negotiate? He decided not to tell his Hedz unless she tricked it out of him, which she probably would.

He didn't have to worry about it because she had seen the whole thing from the ledge in front of their cave.

"What was that all about?"

Bonk sighed. Sometimes it's better to just fess up. "I was out looking for food, and I ran into Grog." Then he mumbled, "He bought my wheel."

Hedz heard that and her eyes went wide. "He bought a rock?"

"Well, sort of."

"Why would he buy something like that? It's worthless! You can't cut with it. You can't dig with it. There's no way a wheel will ever be worth anything!"

"I dunno. I was thinking some day someone might…"

Lump was sitting just inside the cave. She licked her lips. "And he paid you for it? What did he trade? A squirrel? I could go for some nice fat, juicy squirrel right now."

Bonk slid the old lady a hostile look. One of the disadvantages of having two cavewomen in the cave was he was even more outnumbered than he would be otherwise. Hedz didn't need help anyway. Even alone she outnumbered him one to one.

"Um, not exactly."

"A turtle? Turtles have such a nice, gamey taste."

"No," Bonk said, hating where this conversation was headed.

Hedz gave him a bright smile. "You got more than a turtle? My wonderful, brave mate. Maybe you should be a trader instead of a hunter. You have such trading instincts."

"He gave me a check," Bonk blurted.

Hedz looked blank, "A check. Like from Czechoslovakia?"

Bonk couldn't meet her eyes. Lump was smirking

"No, Czechoslovakia hasn't been discovered yet," he mumbled.

Hedz's eyes narrowed, "Tell me, Bonk. What exactly is this check Grog gave you in exchange for your wheel?"

Bonk's face was burning. "It's, um, a leaf. With marking on it."

"A leaf? He gave you a leaf," she said in a deceptively mild voice.

"With marking on it," Bonk said softly, as if the markings imbued particular worth to the leaf.

"So it was a special leaf?" Hedz asked just as softly, but with way more weight to the words.

"Yes," he whispered.

"So what happened to this special leaf with the marking on it?"

"It blew away," his words were barely audible.

"Ah, the leaf blew away. And now you have no leaf with special marking."

"No," he admitted.

"Nor do you have your wheel, which you wasted so much time tinkering with."

"No."

She let the silence build. Then she chuckled. "Well, since you aren't working on your wheel now, I guess you'll have more time to help me clean the cave."

"Um, yeah," Bonk said weakly.

Chapter 16

"All right everyone. Attention please."

Area Wug and his assistant Berp were standing on a large rock overlooking the former Woodhenge, now Charred-henge. Little wisps of smoke drifted from some of the logs. Several dozen cavemen, women and children were spread out around the clearing grunting the morning's news to each other. No one paid the slightest attention to the village elder.

"Hey," Wug shouted.

The tribe kept grunting.

"You all know how to talk!" Wug yelled. "Can we dispense with the animalistic grunting?"

More grunting.

With an exasperated sigh, Wug hauled out an animal hide. He opened its folds and tossed the contents onto the ground in front of the tribe, small objects scattering all over the clearing.

"Yay! Grubs," the kids in the tribe shouted. They pounced on the wriggling bug larvae like kids on candy. As their children scrabbled in the dirt, their parents stopped grunting and looked up.

Wug grinned triumphantly."Works every time."

Then he noticed Bonk. "What happened to your head?"

Bonk colored. "Um, haircut."

"Oh, well okay then." Area Wug dismissed him and turned back to the crowd. "Do I have everyone's attention?"

When he saw he did, he nodded in satisfaction. "Okay, let's get this meeting going." He looked down at his assistant. "What's first on the agenda?"

Berp looked down at the flat rock. It had charcoaled markings on it that meant pretty much nothing. He spoke from memory."We left off the last meeting at duct tape."

"Oh, that's right," Wug said. He looked towards Dork, resident visionary and inventor of stuff. "How are we doing on the duct tape?"

Silence.

"Ahem, Dork," Berp hissed.

Startled, Dork looked up from where he'd been glaring at Bonk.

He noticed everyone looking at him. "What..?"

Sitting in the ashes of his henge had made him freshly angry at the caveman who'd sent months of hard work up in smoke. Forget his realization stone would work better. Forget his excitement over the possibilities of fire. Forget the fresh new supply of charcoal.

"Duct tape," Berp said.

Dork frowned, "What about it?"

Wug shifted his huge bulk, "What's the status?"

"Of what?" Dork asked.

Wug sighed. "Duct tape. You promised you'd invent it."

Dork's angst evaporated. "Oh, yes. Duct tape will be the invention of the universe! The ultimate guy tool!"

"We don't have any tools yet," Berp pointed out.

Dork shook his head. "That's not exactly true. We have pointed sticks."

"Spears," Berp interjected.

"And rocks," Dork continued.

"How are rocks tools?" Wug asked.

"Why they are the perfect hammer, although they perhaps need a handle or something," Dork answered.

"What's a handle?" Bonk asked.

81

Dork spun to answer, "Excellent question. A handle…"
Then he stopped, remembered he was mad at Bonk, and turned
and addressed Wug. "A handle would allow one to…"

"Why not two?" Bonk interrupted.

"What?"

"Why would it allow just one?"

Dork's face was a mix of confusion, "One what?"

"You just said a handle would allow one. Why can't a
handle allow two?"

"A two-handed handle? Genius." Berp said.

"I'm not talking about a two-handed handle," Dork
stammered.

"Actually, you're supposed to be talking about duct tape,"
Wug pointed out.

"Precisely," Dork said, grasping the opportunity to get
back on track. "Anyway, duct tape will be the ultimate guy-tool
…"

"You already said that," Berp interrupted.

"Why can't it be a woman tool?" Hedz asked.

The guys looked at her.

She shrugged, "What?"

"Women don't speak in council," Wug growled.

Silence.

More silence, as the cave people eyed each other
apprehensively.

Then Hedz slowly got to her feet.

Mass intake of breath.

She put one hand on a wide baby serviceable hip.

Holding of said mass intake of breath.

In total synch, she waggled her finger and head and glared,
her beautiful luxurious mustaches swinging spectacularly.
"Excuse me? Did I hear you right?"

Mass ooh'ing and ah'ing.

Then she growled, "What's this 'women don't speak' thing? Who came up with that lovely idea? Who does all the gathering in this tribe? Who puts up with you apes?"

"Hey, she called us apes!" Droog protested.

"Well, I do like climbing trees," Bonk said.

"Oh, well okay then," Droog said.

Hedz wasn't finished. "And who watches the kids while you guys are out trying to run antelopes into blind caverns? Hah! Us. Believe you me, we'd all rather be chasing deer than trying to keep these young ones in check."

"Amen," a woman shouted.

Bonk frowned, "What's an amen?"

Droog scrunched his face, "Is it a man who's an 'a'?"

"Shut up," Hedz snapped. Then she turned back to the crowd. "And just how many of you men ever carried a baby around for almost a year?"

"What's a year?" Bonk asked.

Hedz ignored him. "And periods. Do you get them? Of course you don't. You don't even worry about trying to look nice. Just sit around in your nakedness, watching rock, chasing deer, while we women .." she gestured to the on-looking women who were nodding in delight. "…While we women have to look all nice and pretty for you, while you guys just let yourself go to pot."

Berp picked that moment to burp.

Hedz wheeled on him, 'Exactly my point. Why look at me." Hedz gestured to herself. "You think I haven't noticed all of you men ogling my new beaver skin outfit?"

The guys looked a bit guilty.

Then another woman shouted out, "Woman, you look mighty fine. We have to talk about what you are wearing. What do you call it?"

Hedz smiled broadly, "I call it, clothing. And it tantalizes the male, much more than simply going naked."

Then she turned back to Wug, and shot him a glare. "So I do not want to hear any more of this nonsense about women not speaking in council. Next thing you know, you'll be saying women can't vote. Ridiculous."

And amid enthusiastic applause, mostly from the women, she dropped back to her seat.

Wug stood for a moment, nonplussed.

After a moment, he recovered smoothly. After all, he was almost a politician, adept at taking things in stride. But he couldn't let a challenge to his authority go unquestioned.

He paused and his eyes scanned the women in the crowd. "Actually, I'm kind of glad this came up because we're going to take a vote … today … about whether women should be allowed to vote."

"What?!" Hedz cried. "That's, that's, just so archaic."

"Duh," Wug said. "We're cavemen. What do you expect?"

"Can we women vote in this vote about whether we can vote?" Hedz growled.

"Yes," Wug replied.

Hedz looked around at the women in the tribe. They looked as angry as she felt. She crossed her arms, "Fine, we vote."

The women nodded.

Wug smiled. "Okay, here's how we're going to do this. We don't know how to count yet…"

"What's count?" a caveman yelled.

"My point exactly," Wug continued. "So what we're going to do is simply ask one question."

"And that question?" Hedz asked, sticking a hip out.

"Whether women can vote," Wug said mildly.

"So will we vote by just raising out hands?" Droog asked.

"No, like I said, we haven't invented counting yet," Wug replied. "In order to vote, each member of the tribe will just come down and either stand next to me, which is a vote for 'no,' or stand next to Hedz, which is a vote for 'yes.'

"Are you okay with these rules?" he asked her.

She thought about it. "Can kids vote?"

"Nope, just adults. They had to have reached puberty," Wug said.

Easy enough.

She nodded. "Okay, you're on. Let's do this."

Wug rubbed his hands together and grinned. "All right. I now announce the beginning of the vote."

He looked up at the sea of cavemen and women. "What are you waiting for?"

Everyone looked startled, and then started streaming down to stand next to Wug or Hedz.

When the dust settled, all of the men were standing next to Wug. All of the women were standing next to Hedz.

Everyone, except one. Bonk stood between the two groups, obviously torn.

Wug nodded, "Get over here, son."

Bonk looked at him.

Then his eyes swiveled to his mate and immediately he wished they hadn't. He hadn't seen that look on her face since … well, ever.

Wug immediately realized Bonk's predicament. "Bonk," he said sternly. "Stay strong, man. We need you."

The cavemen behind him started chanting, "We want Bonk. We want Bonk. We want Bonk!" Then they gave him a standing ovation, which was kind of easy, since they were already standing. "Bonk, Bonk, Bonk, Bonk!"

Bonk found himself leaning towards the guys, but another look at his mate stalled him again.

"I could use a new assistant," Wug said coaxingly.

Berp glared.

Hedz glared.

85

Finally, Bonk tore his eyes away from Hedz, and with a big show of hesitancy, and pretending he couldn't see her, he strolled over to the guy's side with the look of someone who just casually chose a direction.

Hedz just nodded, as if confirming something.

Now all of the men were standing with Area Wug and all the women were standing with Hedz.

"We're tied," Hedz said.

Wug looked around. "I don't see it that way."

Hedz's eyes swept over the two groups. "There are an equal amount of men and women. That's a tie."

Wug nodded, "It would appear that way. So the men have prevailed."

Hedz frowned, "I don't get it."

Wug cocked a head. "We outweigh you. That means we win. There's more of us than there is you."

Hedz's eyebrows shot up, "What?"

"Law of the jungle. We're bigger, therefore we win," he said, as if it were obvious.

"This isn't a jungle," Hedz spat.

Wug looked around. "Looks like a jungle to me. Trees, apes. Do you see any condos?"

Hedz frowned, "Condos?"

"Or a Walmart?"

"Walmart?"

"See, no condos, no Walmart. So this is surely a jungle."

Sheez whispered into Hedz's ear, "Are we going to let them get away with this?"

Hedz whispered back, "Don't worry. Women not being able to vote would never last."

Sheez nodded. "I guess you're right."

"Besides, do you have trouble controlling men?" Hedz asked.

Sheez giggled, "No."

"Right, they do whatever we want. So we'll fight later, in public, and in bed. Some of these men might end up regretting taking this stand." She aimed a look at Bonk, who quickly looked away.

Hedz turned back to Wug and smiled graciously, "Fine, we accept the vote."

The chieftain grinned. He was way more relieved than he thought he would be. Hedz was a formidable adversary. He turned back to the crowd.

"Well, okay then. That's settled. Everyone back to your seats."

The cave people headed back. Bonk hesitantly stepped next to Hedz.

She just smiled without humor.

Meanwhile, Wug was back on top of his speechifyng log. "Okay, where did we leave off?"

"Duct tape," Berp quickly said.

"Right, right." He looked back at Dork. "As you were saying…"

Silence.

"Er, Dork?"

"What..?" Dork said. He had been busy checking out Hedz's tantalizing clothing. Then he focused. "Oh, right. Sorry. As I was saying, I'm having a few issues with the duct tape. I found some good adhesive quality tar, but I'm having trouble coming up with a substance that has both fibers and the ripping ability to allow it to be used one-handed. First I tried duck feathers … that makes the most sense, after all, … then bark, and then I tried …"

"Well, you just keep trying," Wug interrupted. He was aware that Dork would go on if not stopped. He looked down at Berp, "Okay, what's next?"

"God," Berp said.

"Oh, right," Wug said. He turned back to the crowd, and announced, "As discussed last meeting, it's high time we got ourselves a god."

"Why?" Droog drawled.

Wug glared at him, "Because we do, man."

"I think he's right," Yup said. Yup was a short stocky caveman who was famous only for having the deepest belly button pit in the community.

Droog turned a caustic look at Yup, "And why's that?"

"We need someone to pray to," Yup replied.

Droog sighed, "I'm still not hearing a reason."

Wug stood, "We need a god who will give us things."

"Like refrigeration?" Dork asked.

"What?" Wug asked.

"Refrigeration. We could keep our food cold that way," Dork explained.

"Why would we want to do that?" Droog asked.

Bonk raised a hand, "Actually, I recently found out I like my food warm."

"Refrigeration would let us keep food longer," Dork said.

"I don't want to keep it longer. I want to eat it." Lunk leaned against what was left of one of the log columns.

Dork rolled his eyes. Sometimes explaining things to the other cavemen exhausted his patience. "Look, if we can keep food longer, we can store excess food to use when food is scarce."

The other cavemen just looked blank.

Then Berp piped up. "If we had a god, we could just ask God for food when we need it. So we wouldn't need to store it."

Deth nodded in agreement. "Plus storing food is dangerous. It just attracts predators."

"And rats," Tacks added.

"Actually, I like rats," Grog said. "They're a bit chewy, and they fight back, but there's a really nice taste to them."

Feeling control of the meeting slipping away from him, Wug harrumphed loudly.

Everyone kept talking.

"Everyone quiet!"

The buzzing continued.

"I'm going to count to three," Wug threatened.

That got their attention.

Bonk looked up. "What's that mean?"

"I'm going to count. And when I hit three, you'd all better have settled down."

"What's a three?" Bonk asked.

Wug snapped his fingers, "Crap, that's right, I forgot, we don't have arithmetic yet." "Anyway, listen up everyone. You're all right. A god could give us whatever we wanted, whether it be food, good weather, protection from animals …"

"Actually, fire works for protection," Bonk interrupted.

This got everyone's attention. They had heard about the fire, and the ashes smeared all over their butts were proof of its power. But none of them had ever seen fire up close, or even more, carried it. They were in bit of awe over Bonk's accomplishment. And that he had used fire to face down two dire wolves, burn down the henge and cook a living creature was just a bit overwhelming.

"Yeah, when used in the right hands," Dork said, glowering at Bonk. He still was miffed about the henge.

"Fire seems pretty useful, if we could just figure out how to store it," Hedz said.

"We could ask God to help," Berp ventured.

"We don't have a God yet," Droog reminded him.

"Oh, yeah, that's right," Berp said.

"Okay, so what do we do?"

Having experimented extensively with fire, Bonk felt vastly qualified to venture an expert opinion. "It doesn't store well in water."

"That's helpful," Droog said sarcastically.

...

(There's no absolute proof, but this may be the first recorded use of the art of sarcasm by humans. In fact, animals to this day still don't get the concept of sarcasm, with the possible exception of the common housecat, for which there are certain instances where they might be employing this type of humor.)

...

"Not really," Hedz frowned.

...

(Proving that the first observers of sarcasm didn't quite understand the concept either. It would be awhile before sarcasm would be accepted as a higher level of humor over the lower but more hilarious forms of humor, such as getting bonked on the head by a club or tripping and falling down a cavern.)

...

"Actually, fire seems to work best with wood," she continued.

"Interesting," Wug said, stroking his thick, lustrous eyebrow hair. He had to keep it greased with animal fat so it wouldn't fall in his face. "We will have to capture some of this fire so we can experience its wonderfulness ourselves."

"Just don't touch it with your hands," Bonk said, holding up a blistered finger.

Everyone ooh'ed and ah'ed appreciatively.

"Okay, back to the God-thing," Wug announced. "I call a meeting up at the top of the big hill so we can pray for and receive our God. We'll meet at the arrival of the day disk." He paused, and swept a glower across his audience. "Attendance is mandatory."

Everyone groaned.

"Er, I was sort of planning on sleeping in tomorrow," Tack complained.

"What's a tomorrow?" Deth asked.

"I dunno," Tack said sheepishly.

Then Lunk spoke up, "I'm feeling a bit TGIF-ish, too."

"What's a TGIF-ish?" Deth asked.

"I don't know," Lunk responded. "But I've had a tough week and need a couple days to recharge."

"What's a week?" Deth asked.

"What are days?" Berp asked.

"I dunno," Lunk said. "But, well, you know…" he shrugged helplessly.

"I feel the same way," Tack said.

"Yeah, me, too," Bonk said.

"We've been hunting a lot," Deth piped up.

"And gathering," Sheez added, as usual drawing a few looks from the on-looking cave guys. Sheez was a gorgeous young cavewoman with a sweet looking unibrow.

"And wheeling," Grog added, ignoring Bonk's glare.

Being a fine politician, Area Wug knew how to ride prevailing winds. "Fine. We meet when the day disk is halfway across the sky."

Without another word, he wheeled and walked towards his cave, confident they would obey.

Berp stood up, and announced, "This meeting is adjourned."

As Hedz stood to leave, Sheez strolled over, followed by several cave girls and by more than one caveman eyes. Sheeze's many female parts moved the way female parts do, in a way that guys like to look at. When Bonk saw her coming he quickly sucked in his gut. Hedz decided for his sake not to notice.

"What's up?" she asked the curvaceous cave girl.

"Hi, um, Hedz. I was…" she started.

"We were…" one of the other cave girls corrected.

Sheez looked back, nodded, and went on, "We were wondering … um…" she blushed, much to the delight of the cave guys loitering ostensibly to admire the burnt henges when really all they wanted was to ogle nubile cave girls.

"About what you're wearing," another finished.

"The furs?" Hedz asked, gesturing to her beaver fur outfit.

Sheez's eyes swept over the concealing furs. "Yes. It's um, very nice."

"Provocative?" Hedz asked.

Sheez shuffled her feet, her eyes downcast demurely, "Um, yes."

Smiling, Hedz asked, "You want to know how to do it, right?"

"Yes, please," Sheez said.

"Please," her little band chorused.

Hedz smacked Bonk, whose eyes had strayed to some pretty girl parts, "Okay, meet me at the riverbed at first light. We have things to talk about."

Then, taking Bonk's hairy arm, she steered him towards the cave.

Chapter 17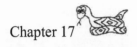

The next morning arrived with light too weak to chase all of the darkness out of the sky. Gray-black rainclouds rode the swift currents of air, crisscrossing the landscape with some clouds rocketing in one direction with other higher clouds going the exact opposite direction.

Bonk stood at the mouth of the cave. He had a rock in each hand and was clapping them together and nodding to the beat.

"*Boo, ya ra, da, ruck,*" he chanted.

"*Ya, da, bick da bong...*
Wu, muck rah fa doov...
Hum, da, rip we dah..."

Hedz strolled out of the cave, stretching sleepily. "What are you doing?" The kids were still in the sleeping pit sprawled together in sleep like a family of ferrets.

"Practicing."

Hedz watched small bits of rock chips bounce off the ground. "Practicing what?"

"I'm trying out for the band," he said, still banging rocks. He was swinging his head, long hair whipping.

"The what?"

"The band. I'm gonna be in a rock band. Listen to my song."

"*Boo, ya ra, da, ruck,*
"*Ya, da bick da bong...*
Wu, muck rah fa doov...
Hum, da, rip we dah..."

93

Hedz watched him for another moment, a hint of a smile playing at the corners of her mouth. "I think you should make them rhyme."

"What?"

Then a rock split in half, crushing Bonk's fingers.

"Aaahh!" Bonk dropped the rocks and jammed the injured fingers into his mouth, trying to suck the pain away. After a moment, he pulled them out and critically examined them to determine the severity of the injury. No blood, the skin wasn't broken. But they were red and throbbing. He stuck them back into his mouth.

He wasn't seriously hurt, so Hedz's attention went to the broken pieces of rock. Bending over, she picked up a hand-sized shard. It was relatively flat, thicker on one side than the other, the thin side tapering to a flat but very sharp edge. She drew a finger along the edge and it nearly sliced through her thick calluses.

If light bulbs had been invented, one would have gone off over her head. Smiling, she slipped the stone under one of the rawhide ties holding her furs on.

Then she answered, "Rhyming. It's when different words sound similar to each other."

"Mmph?" Bonk asked around a mouth full of fingers.

"Like this. Boo rhymes with who, which rhymes with moo."

Bonk's eyes widened and he pulled his digits from his mouth. "That's cool!"

"Which rhymes with fool. And tool," she added pointedly.

"What's a tool?" Bonk asked. "We were talking about that at the Guys Meeting today and I wasn't clear on the concept."

Hedz ignored that. "Now if you're going to make a song…"

"What's a song?" Bonk interrupted.

"A song is what you were creating. When you chant in a cadence in rising, falling or extended pitch."

Bonk nodded. "So it's not just beating, tapping or slamming things together."

"Right," Hedz said. "You can do both singing and playing objects, or either in rhythm. And rhyming rhythms sound more pleasing to the ear. Like you were chanting this,

"Boo, ya ra, da, ruck,
"Ya, da , bick da bong...
Wu, muck rah fa doov...
Hum, da, rip we dah..."

She paused and said, "Do it a bit different, like...

"U arh a nete shmuk,
"an git inn dah muck...
Be ah gi just wong...
Dis iz dah fust song."

Bonk hopped up and down. "That's just totally cool," he cried. Then he stopped hopping. "But the words that sound alike were at the end of the lines. Why not put them at the beginning?"

"I don't know," she replied. "It just sounds better. Why don't you keep practicing and watch the kids while I go down to the river?"

Bonk nodded his agreement. His lips were moving as he repeated the words to himself backwards. Back then people had better memories because they didn't have any way to write things down. That and because they had more available memory because they didn't have to remember where they left their car keys, cell phones or their password for Facebook.

Hedz went back into the cave, grabbed some furs, other animal parts and plant bulbs. She smooched the kids who stirred sleepily without waking when her moustaches ticked their cheeks.

As she passed Bonk, he said, "You're right. The rhyming sounds better at the end. Weird." He shook his head in amazement.

"Of course I'm right," Hedz responded. "I'm a female."

"Huh? What's that got to do with it?"

"Fe' means 'smarter than,'" she said with a straight face.

Then she headed down the slope towards the river, butt swaying.

"Smarter than?" Bonk repeated behind her. Then his brain shut down for a moment as he was hypnotized by the swaying motion of his mate's rear.

As she neared the path at the bottom of the slope, his brain kicked back into gear, "Hah, I get it. Fe-male. Smarter than male…wait."

Pause.

"Hey!"

Hedz smiled and headed to the riverbank.

Chapter 18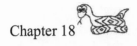

"I'm hungry," Gop said, emerging from the cave.

Bonk was sitting on a femur that a springtime rockslide had unearthed next to the cave mouth. Bonk, who had seen many dead creatures in his life, had never encountered an animal this big. The huge bone dwarfed that of mastodons and even the ground sloth. It was even bigger than the huge fish that had beached one summer. The entire village had lived on its flesh for weeks before the meat went bad.

He had seen other colossal bones buried or half buried in the sides of crumbling cliffs, and considered himself lucky to have never met the beasts when they were still living. He wondered idly if they were man, beast, or like the Meefs, something in between.

"Um, I said I'm hungry," Gop repeated.

"Oh, sorry. Here," he reached behind him. "I traded some spears with Droog for some badger legs. He hates making spears."

"You mean pointed sticks," Gop giggled.

"No, spears," Bonk protested.

"They're sticks with ends sharpened by rubbing on rocks."

"No, they're sapling trunks. It takes talent and patience to find the right trees, cut them without splintering the wood, strip off the branches and leaves and file them down."

She grinned. "Whatever." Then she bit into badger, sharp incisors ripping through hide and tendons.

Bonk watched his daughter chew. "So what's on your schedule for the day?"

Gop swallowed a hunk of meat. "I've got a pretty full day. First I have to go meet mom down at the river. Then I'm going to interview prospective mates."

Bonk's eyebrows shot up, "Really?"

"Yep," Gop said. She bit off more meat, chewed and said, "I figure on maybe two or three."

"Interviews?"

"No, mates," she said with her cheeks full.

"What are you talking about?"

Gop swallowed, then grinned, "I'm going to have two or three mates."

"Um, we haven't invented divorce yet," Bonk said.

"Who said anything about divorce? I'm going to have two or three at the same time. Maybe four."

"Four?" Bonk blinked. He could barely handle a single mate.

"Yep. One to do the hunting, one to clean the cave, one to watch the children and maybe an extra one to be my own personal mechanic if we ever invent cars."

"But…"

"Oh, wait, and maybe a fifth one for sex."

"But, but…"

"Then again, maybe all of them for sex," she said pensively.

"But, but…"

"After all," she said brightly, "Who said men are the only ones who can have harems?"

"But, but…"

"It's not like there are any rules yet," she continued.

Chapter 19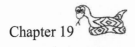

Sheez and several other cave girls were at the riverbank when Hedz arrived. Hedz looked around warily for the huge croc. It wasn't in the river. Ah, there it was, lurking in its nest in the small marshy lagoon, a baleful eye watching the humans. After its last encounter with cavemen, it wasn't inclined to venture far from its nest. Maybe this meant the croc decided to eliminate cave people as potential food sources. Or maybe not. Hedz suspected humans would be back on the menu once her babies left the nest.

"Hi," Hedz said to the girls.

"Hi!" they chorused, their eyes fixed on Hedz's beaver fur outfit.

A voice came from behind Hedz. "Hey, did you start yet?"

Hedz turned. Gop was trotting towards them.

"Nope, you're in time."

A small leaf blew across Gop's path. It had markings on it, so she picked it up. She studied the small leaf. Then she shook her head in puzzlement and tossed it back on the ground, where a small breeze caught it and dribbled it away.

The girls were sitting on the bank, naked without the realization of being nude. But now, with Hedz standing in front of them, clad in fur, they were just getting the first inklings of 'something.' Their hearts fluttered with excitement and the prescient notion that maybe makeup and high heels wouldn't be too far in the future.

Hedz was pleased with their rapt attention.

"Okay, ladies," she said, dumping furs and plant bulbs on the ground. The furs included a small corpse involuntarily donated by a rat. She had clobbered it that morning as it was sniffing baby Eff, its tiny rodent brain evaluating the possibility of consuming an earlobe for breakfast. Hedz had turned the tables on the rat.

"Okay, we're going to start with something I call 'cleaning," Hedz said, picking up one of the bulbs.

"Cleaning? What's that?" Yerba asked.

Hedz stepped into the river, casting a quick precautionary look at the crocodile. The croc was watching her attentively, but made no attempt to move.

As the water went over Hedz's knees, the girls gasped in amazement.

The water's cool velvety touch caressed her legs, tickling the fur on her calves.

"Watch this," Hedz murmured. With the bulb in her hands, she plunged them into the water, eliciting more excited oohs and ahs from the on-looking girls. Then she rubbed the bulb vigorously, releasing the liquid from its fibers. Then she took her hands out of the water, still rubbing the bulb, showing them the white suds bubbling up from her hands. She rubbed the suds onto her arms, releasing dirt and mud from their longtime homes on her skin.

The girls tittered.

Hedz lifted a shapely leg onto a small log that had gotten caught in the current. Smearing the bubbles onto her leg she dipped it back in the river to rinse. When she lifted the leg again, it was smooth, glistening, black leg hairs shining with cleanliness.

The girls shrieked in delight.

Then Hedz untied the strips of leather holding her beaver fur on, and slid completely out of the pelt. She looked more nude than any human had ever looked.

The girls gasped.

"She's so ... naked," Sheez whispered.

"More naked than anyone, ever," Gop breathed, amazed at the accomplishments of her own mother.

"Imagine the effects this would have on a guy," another girl said.

"Whoa," they chorused.

Meanwhile, Hedz continued cleaning, soaping her front, then her back. She glanced over at the croc to make sure it was keeping its distance, and satisfied, dipped under the surface.

When she disappeared, the girls jumped up, ready to ... they didn't know. Save her?

Suddenly Hedz popped back up, the soap was rinsed away and her skin glistened like a dolphin.

"Whoa," the girls shouted.

Then they started clapping.

Sheez looked at her friend Phut. "What are we doing?"

Phut was clapping vigorously, "Huh?"

"Why are we slapping our palms together?"

Phut looked down at her hands, which were, in fact, slapping together.

She frowned, "Um, I don't know. But I felt like doing it."

"Yeah, me too," Sheez replied. Then she forgot about it and kept clapping at the woman standing triumphantly in the water.

Hedz soaped her hair and her mustache, which released a small amount of grease and oils to drift down the river like a miniature BP Amoco oil slick. Then she turned her attention to the beaver furs and plunged them into the river, soaping and soaking them. She rinsed the suds, shook the excess water loose and tossed the pelts onto the bank to dry. The girls could see how the furs repelled the water, leaving them glossy and shiny.

101

Then Hedz climbed out of the river, water streaming down her smooth, glistening skin. No, not just smooth and glistening. Her skin was clean.

Sheez gently took Hedz's arm. Hedz just watched, a quirk playing at the corner of her mouth. Sheez ran a finger slowly down the arm, watching the water squeegee in rivulets down the brown skin. She frowned when she saw the mud tracked by her own dirty finger onto the previously pristine skin.

Then she sniffed. A wisp of a smile ghosting her face, she sniffed deeper, drawing the clean soapy smell up into her olfactory senses.

Her smile grew slowly, lazily. Good thing no cave guy was around because the wicked, sensual look on the pretty girl's face would have done things to his brain.

"I want this," Sheez said quietly.

"Yes," Hedz agreed. "We have been dirty too long."

She tossed soap bulbs to the girls, who squealed and eagerly snatched at the valuable plants.

Before they could leap into the river, Hedz stopped them.

"But first, you must learn clothing," she said.

Taking her new sharp stone, she proceeded to skin the rat. The sharp stone worked much better than the sharp sticks she had used to pry the beaver from its fur.

Chapter 20

Grog pushed the wheel through the forest glade, marveling at how smoothly the heavy stone moved through the matted leaves. He had to give credit to Bonk for the quality of his work. It crackled and crunched over leaves and branches smashing them effortlessly.

Then he realized he was thirsty, so he leaned the wheel against a tree and untied a gourd from around his waist. The gourd, which he had purchased that morning with a personal check, was hollow and filled with water. Haird, the cavewoman he bought it from, hadn't wanted to admit she didn't know what a check was, so she taken it with the same puzzlement Bonk had.

The whole check-thing was pretty slick, so Grog resolved to actually create the system he was pretending to use. Some day, perhaps. In the meantime, it was easy and convenient to buy tangible objects using common leaves with charcoal scratched on them.

His thirst slaked, he let the gourd drop back down to his waist and tipped the wheel back onto its edge. As the wheel spun ahead, he pondered its possible uses. He'd tried using it as a table for his breakfast. It had been okay to eat off, but was inconvenient to lift it back onto its edge afterward.

So while he waited for inspiration to strike, he wheeled around the village, drawing the admiration of his fellow cavemen. Grog accepted their compliments with equanimity, not bothering to admit that Bonk was the actual inventor or that he'd swindled him out of the invention.

The wheel had to have some kind of useful purpose. He halfway wished he'd gotten Bonk's ideas about it before he absconded with it.

There was a patch of moss ahead, and he rolled the stone though the soft green plants, noticing idly the rolling stone didn't gather any moss. Then he got to the hill, and started rolling the heavy stone up its incline. For a reason he could not figure out, the stone suddenly became resistant to his efforts. Grunting, he pushed harder and the stone started rolling again.

He paused, leaning into the stone since it seemed to want to roll the opposite direction he was headed. He wondered if maybe he could market it as an exercise machine for cave people to store their clothes on if they ever started wearing them.

Nah, he'd never met a fat caveman. How could humans ever possibly get fat? Food was scarce and they got all the exercise they needed either running after prey, or trying to avoid being prey. Exercise would never catch on. Especially repetitive lifting of heavy objects for no particular reason.

He looked up the hill. He wasn't even halfway.

He looked back down the hill and as he did, the rock shifted, clearly eager to go that direction.

Then inspiration hit him. He would ride the wheel down the hill!

Holding onto the edges, he slid along its side, gripping ridges rough from Bonk's chiseling. The wheel was about eight inches thick and as tall as Grog. Grog had no concept of weight, but he was strong and capable, so he wrestled until he was uphill of the wheel. He could feel the precariousness of his position. The weight was such that it would take very little to launch both wheel and caveman down the hill.

Grog gritted his teeth, and playing tug of war with gravity, considered just how he might scamper on top for the ride down the hill. Finally, his grip began to give and the wheel started moving. With the decision wrested from him, he decided to just launch on top and ride down the hill in majestic glory and splendiforousness.

Before he could, the wheel started rolling, lifting him from the ground. Oh joy, he wouldn't have to try to jump after all. He clung on and as he reached its apex, he stood.

One of the good things about Grog was he was a quick thinker. He sucked as a slow thinker, and his mental faculties simply worked much better under stress. He quickly realized he couldn't just sit on top and ride, and if he didn't do something he would be carried right under the wheel. With a coward's instinct to know which way to run, he started running the opposite way the wheel was rolling.

As the wheel picked up speed and momentum, it occurred to him that by running the opposite direction the wheel was going, he was assisting the rock's progress in the other direction. Hopefully, some physics geek would be born in the near future who could explain. In the meantime, he had enough on his mind just keeping his balance as the stone went faster and faster. Then faster and faster.

Soon Grog was running with every bit of speed he possessed, focused on keeping his balance on the thin edge of the wheel.

They zoomed down the hill past a couple of stunned cavemen. When Grog saw them, he fixed what he hoped looked like a jaunty and confident smile on his face.

Then the rock hit a natural ramp and Grog went airborne.

Chapter 21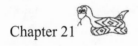

Area Wug slid from his cave, massive shoulders brushing the worn smooth walls of the entrance. He took note of the gray sky. It was going to rain again. Then he shrugged, rain or sun, they would still meet. The issue of God was too important to cancel over something as mundane as inclement weather.

Behind him someone coughed politely and said, "Ahem."

"Eeeekk!" Wug shrieked, launching an incredible three inches into the air.

He landed with a thud, nearly setting off a level three earthquake. He whirled as quickly as his huge body allowed, his centrifugal motion sucking a small current of air into the substantial wake and disturbing the flight patterns of several of his personal flies.

A greasy little caveman stood there, seemingly unaffected by the glower Wug shot at him for nearly scaring him out of his back hair.

"Who are you?" Wug thundered, deliberately dropping his voice several octaves to make up for his girly shriek.

The caveman grinned a grin that would in later years be planted on the faces of used car salesman, televangelists and teenaged boys meeting their girls' parents for the first time. It was nearly a weapon in itself.

"I'm Lob," he said in a rich voice belying his sneaky manner.

Wug frowned. "Lob?"

"Yep," Lob said. He bent over and picked up a couple of dead rabbits Wug hadn't noticed until that point. They were tied together with small vines.

Lob held the rabbits out.

Wug, didn't move to take them.

"Here, take them," Lob insisted with the flashy grin that made Wug feel like guarding his wallet. "They're free."

Wug hesitantly took the rabbits but the other caveman didn't immediately let go. The rabbits were stretched out between the two cavemen like a furry tug of war.

"There is just one condition though," Lob said, still not letting go.

"And what's that?" Wug said suspiciously, not letting go of his end either. Food was scarce and not something lightly relinquished.

"Well, nothing specific," Lob replied. "Just whenever you're going to make a decision that affects the village, I'd just like the opportunity to give my input. You know, like an advisor."

Wug thought and couldn't see the harm. "Well, okay. But just as an advisor."

Lob grinned again, and let go of his end of the rabbits. "Perfect. Just an advisor."

He turned and scampered up the hill. "I'll be in touch."

Chapter 22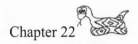

Wug watched Lob disappear up the hill and then someone behind him coughed politely. "Ahem."

"Eeeekk!" Wug shrieked, once again launching a good quarter foot into the air.

He raised a fist to pound the culprit and paused. It was his personal toady, Berp.

"Oh, it's you," Wug growled.

"Good morning, Sir," Berp chirped.

"Yeah, whatever." He crooked a thumb up the hill where Lob had disappeared. "Didja see that guy?"

Berp looked up the hill. "What guy?"

"Never mind." Perhaps he'd imagined it. Then he felt the weight of the rabbits and looked down. Nope, he hadn't imagined it. The little guy was weird, but any caveman knew how valuable food was, and wouldn't turn down a free meal. He wondered idly what the fellow had meant about consulting. He mentally shrugged. Probably nothing important. He looked over the colorless landscape. He didn't need a weatherman to know rain would be coming soon.

As he looked over the valley, his adrenaline levels were ebbing from their earlier spikes, and he gave a massive yawn.

Since yawns are contagious, Berp yawned, too.

Wug finished the yawn, scratched under his arm, dislodging some disgruntled lice, and said, "I can't wait until we invent Starbucks."

"Yessir. Coffee would be a nice way to start a day," Berp agreed.

"So what's first on the agenda?" Wug picked at a scab on his finger.

Berg went to answer, and then he saw something fly overhead.

"Look, a UFO."

Wug's head whipped around, "A what?"

"An unidentified flying object!" Berp said.

A spinning disk soared overhead with a caveman riding on top, legs pumping frantically and a rictus grin pasted to his face.

"Who's that?" Wug asked.

"I dunno" Berp responded.

Then the flying object broke into two UFO's. One plummeted to earth, landing with a jolt, and continued rolling down the hill. The other object dropped, bounced with a lot of groaning and moaning, and tumbled down the hill, arms and legs flopping.

Wug and Berg watched the two objects roll down the hill, across the path and splash into the river.

When Grog's head popped up from the water, they quickly lost interest.

"Are you hungry?" Wug asked.

"Sure thing," Berg replied, eyeing the rabbits.

"Okay, go get us something while I put these rabbits away for later," Wug said, thrusting them into the cave.

"Oh, okay," Berg said, dolefully watching what could have been breakfast disappear. "I think I know where I can get some baby armadillo."

"Sounds good," Wug said. "I love food that comes in its own bowl."

Chapter 23

Grog groggily shook his head. His face was buried in sand and his body fully immersed in the river.

The river?

"Aargh," he cried, spitting out sand and scrambling out of the dangerous shallows before something horrible happened along, like maybe a croc, giant carnivorous river otter or … shudder … cleanliness.

On the bank, he took measure. He was covered with wet sand but nothing appeared broken. Then he heard laughing behind him and turned. Two cavemen laughing and pointing. Correction, nothing physical was broken, just his pride.

He decided to ignore his troglodyte spectators.

Okay, so now where was the wheel?

Ah, there it was, in the reeds of the shallow water. A couple small fish were nosing it curiously and a submerged frog watched with amphibian boredom waiting for something more edible to show up.

He swept his gaze up and down the river, looking for predators. He didn't see any, so he splashed back into the water, gritting his teeth at the revolting feeling of water washing dirt from his legs. The stone was in about a foot of water. Well, he knew two things now. Obviously a wheel would never make good transportation. And it didn't float.

But he still wanted it. After all, he'd paid for it. Sort of.

Mustering courage, he reached into the slick water, trying not to think how the wet felt like some kind of creepy-crawly creature climbing on his skin, and he grabbed onto the side of the wheel. Grunting with the effort, he wrestled it back to shore, rolled it up the embankment, and onto the path.

Just then, he heard the cavemen yelling.

"What?" he snapped. He'd given them enough entertainment for the morning.

"Grrr," they responded.

Then he realized cavemen hadn't answered him. No caveman could create such a low, animalistic sound.

Slowly, he turned around and looked into the hungry gaze of a cave badger. The badger, a close relative of the weasel and mink (though they rarely went to the same family reunions) was a short, squatty creature the size of a small bear with huge shoulders, wide powerful jaws and talon-like nails perfect for digging a den or eviscerating tasty cavemen. It had a black band crossing its face, so it looked a bit like a raccoon on steroids.

"Erk," Grog squawked.

The badger growled again and took a step towards him. The wide shaggy creature radiated strength and hostility.

"Erk," Grog croaked again, wishing he had a weapon, any weapon.

The badger took another stiff step, talons ripping a trench into the compacted dirt of the trail. Grog knew the scimitar-like talons would do worse to him.

Up the hill, the cavemen were yelling and screaming, trying to distract the badger. But the tan beast royally ignored them, its hunting gaze locked on Grog.

Grog maneuvered so the wheel was between them. The cagey badger tried to circle around and Grog spun to keep the wheel between them.

The badger stopped circling and snarled. Then it rushed.

Grog squealed, and shoved the wheel at the badger. The heavy stone struck a glancing blow on the badger's face and slammed onto its thick front paws. It yelped and leaped back. Then it looked at Grog with a startled look on its fuzzy face.

With nothing but the fallen wheel between him and the badger, Grog screeched defiance at the predator. Something worked because the badger turned and shuffled away as fast as its bowlegged gait could take it.

Grog watched its retreat in total amazement.

Now he knew what use there was for a wheel.

Defense.

Chapter 24

The platypus is the Frankenstein of the animal kingdom. An egg-laying mammal, it has the body of a chubby muskrat, no visible ears, webbed feet of an otter, tail of a beaver, and a duck's bill. It looks like something put together by some kids playing with an animalistic Mr. Potato Head. In fact, when European naturalists first encountered the platypus, they would suspect it was a hoax.

The platypus was swimming up the river, pulling itself with its front feet. Its head swept left and right, its sensitive bill searching for the electromagnetic signature of its prey. Its eyes and nose were closed and it hunted with its bill alone.

Finally, it detected a crayfish, and the platypus's head darted forward, neatly snaring the crustacean and storing it in a cheek pouch. A platypus has to eat nearly twenty percent of its body weight every day.

The platypus surfaced and made for the rocks. When it reached shore, it pulled onto the rocks and climbed on top, walking on knuckles to keep from injuring its fragile webbed feet.

That's when the eagle hit.

Huge talons dug into the platypus's thick fur and the eagle launched back into the air.

At that moment, the platypus wished for one more animal part, wings.

It screamed as it went airborne.

Chapter 25

"Let's go, let's go," Berp shouted. "It's going to rain any time now."

The villagers were streaming up the hill from their caves, grumbling as they cast eyes on the black skies.

"Why don't we just postpone?" Droog grumped.

"Don't be a wimp," Berp said sarcastically.

"What's a wimp?" Droog asked.

"I think it's something you hit people with," Deth said, feet scrabbling up the rocky incline.

"No, that's not right," Dork said. "That's a whip, and I haven't invented it yet, though it's on the drawing board."

"A wimp," Berp said caustically, "is a guy who acts like he isn't a guy."

"You mean a woman?" Tork said, chewing on a rat kabob as he climbed.

"I like women," Droog said.

"No, a wimp is not a woman," Berp said.

"Good thing," Bonk said. "I wouldn't want to be attracted to Droog."

"Speaking of women, where are they?" Berp was frowning, looking around. Most of the villagers climbing the hill were cavemen and cave children.

"Hedz has most of them down at the river," Bonk replied. "She said they'd be here on time for the meeting."

The cave guys and cave children spread out in the clearing, racing for any shelter against the oncoming rain. Bonk and

Droog found an overhang next to a large stone. The stone was rectangular, weighing several tons.

"Where did this stone come from?" Droog asked, patting the rock as if to reassure himself it actually existed. "It wasn't here yesterday."

"I dunno," Bonk replied. "Dork got it here somehow. He said it was for something he called a stone henge."

Droog shook his head. "That's dude's slightly weird."

Area Wug was standing on a pile of logs from the recently demised Woodhenge.

"Attention everyone," he cried.

They looked at him.

He looked back, and a dark look went across his face.

"We're missing people," he growled.

"Um, they're coming," Bonk said.

Wug's glower went to Bonk. "When?"

Droog was looking past them, and then his eyes went wide. "Oh. My. God."

Wug cut him a glance. "We don't have a god yet."

Bonk followed Droog's gaze, and then his mouth dropped open.

Wug followed both gazes, and then his eyes widened.

The rest of the villagers' eyes swung over, too, and their eyes, too, went to perfect Visine-receiving positions.

For just then, from the small copse of trees lining the clearing, a procession of women came down the small path, led by Hedz.

They looked, well, …

…different.

....

The eagle winged for altitude, a struggling platypus in its talons. The platypus spat the still wriggling crayfish at the eagle, but the effort was futile and the crayfish just tumbled towards the fast moving earth below. The eagle never noticed, heading for its nest in the hills, barely distracted by the wind playing on a head devoid of feathers.

Chapter 26

Hedz led a group of women out of the woods.

This wasn't remarkable in itself. What was remarkable was the women, mostly younger, had been thoroughly scrubbed. Gop, Sheez and the other girls had had their hair cleansed of oily dirt, the wind fetchingly blowing long locks of hair like a Revlon shampoo commercial. Their faces were brown and smooth, flush and glowing with excitement and vitality. Hair had been combed with eel vertebrae, fingernails filed smooth by stone, skin exfoliated with lava rocks, teeth picked clean by thorns, hair conditioned with chunked, peeled cactus. Garlands of flowers were draped around their slim necks and braided into their hair and mustaches.

But there was more.

Each of the women was clothed in furs, artfully tied in such a way that the watching cavemen were treated to a sight that no caveman had ever, ever, ever…

…ever …

… seen before.

A sight that would delight and bedevil man forever after …

Cleavage.

....

The platypus had been stunned by the blow to his shoulders and had just been struggling feebly. It had totally forgotten that nature, that while showing its sense of humor in its Frankenstein-ish creation, had given the platypus a gift unique to mammals. Then it remembered the poisonous spur on its hind foot.

It struggled in the eagle's grasp, futilely trying to stab the huge eagle.

Chapter 27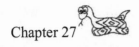

"What's that?" Droog said, absentmindedly wiping a bit of drool.

"I…I …" Bonk replied, his gaze fixated on the enticing new valley that had somehow appeared upon Hedz's chest.

Wug stammered, "Meeting, um, meeting. We're meeting…"

Seeing they were the center of attention, the women blushed, lowering their heads demurely.

The rest of the cavemen were transfixed.

Nudity, they were used to. Heck, they saw it every day.

But the absence of nudity.

Well, wow.

Rapt silence.

"Sorry we're late," Hedz said quietly, her voice carrying to eager ears.

"Um," Wug replied.

The women paraded single-file into the center of the clearing, where they spread out until they were standing in a line facing the tribe.

They were met with stunned silence.

"Well?" Sheez said, spreading her arms out wide, exposing her deep ravine of visual pleasure. "What do you think?"

Jaws dropped.

The women smiled coyly.

Being women, they knew they should always keep their audience wanting, so without further voguing, they broke up to rejoin their families.

As Hedz approached, Bonk's breathing quickened and his heart started doing strange things.

"Uh, how would you, um, like to go back to the cave?" he gasped.

Hedz just smiled and sat demurely next to him, a pleasant scent shadowing her, sending strange new signals to Bonk's olfactory nerves, which prior to this had only been used for following game.

"You smell …"

He wasn't sure how to complete this sentence, in that he didn't know what she smelled like. Only that it was doing weird things to him.

"No, that's okay. You boys have some meeting or something you want to do," she responded, amusement coloring her voice whatever color amusement is. She waved a languid hand, "Go ahead and get to it."

Bonk looked up at Wug whose head was swiveling back and forth from Hedz to Sheez.

Finally Wug gave up, and collected himself. He looked around for his toady.

Berp's eyes were in fact a bit toady, and were focused on the girls. Wug clouted him on the head, causing Berp to bite his tongue, which had been hanging out, catching wind.

The tongue flipped back and Berp clapped hands to his mouth.

"Wpfz?"

"What are you doing ogling girls when we have important village work to do?"

"Well, technically, we aren't a village, you know," Berp lisped with his hurt tongue. "Cities, towns, that's all future

120

stuff. At best, we might be a loose community or a gathering of families or something."

"I don't care about that. Until they figure out social stuff like that, we're a village. I declare it so."

"We could start taxing," a voice suddenly said from the other side of Wug. He would have scared the pants off Wug had there been any pants to scare off.

Wug turned and glared. It was the little fellow Lob.

Lob gave him a tiny wave, and continued, "And once you start taxing, I could give you stuff to entice you to lower taxes on the rich so all of the burden is on the middle class."

Wug frowned, "Stuff, what stuff?"

Lob whipped out a couple of dead ground squirrels. "Like this."

Wug licked his lips, "Yum, I love ground squirrels."

"Take them," Lob said, shoving them into Wug's non-protesting hands. "No strings. I promise."

Then he hopped off the logs and vanished.

Wug looked at the squirrels. He couldn't see any strings. Shrugging, he turned back to the crowd, which was buzzing like an upset hornet nest. He raised two massive arms, calling for silence.

"Okay, attention everyone," he shouted.

He got no one's attention.

Wug frowned and nodded to Berg who leaned over and grabbed a handful of gravel. He flung it into the crowd.

"Hey!"

"Ouch!"

"Jorj!"

Berg ignored the insults and grinned, "Thank you, thank you. It's time to commence with today's meeting."

He stepped backward, ceding authority to Area Wug, who stepped forward, a politician's grin spreading across his face. "Thank you all for coming," he trumpeted.

"Like you gave us any choice," Droog grumbled.

Wug ignored him. "As we discussed at the last meeting, it is time to make our lives easier!"

This sounded good, so a few cave people nodded.

"We shouldn't have to work so hard!" Wug thundered.

A small bit of real thunder punctuated his words, and a few of the cave people looked nervously up at the oppressive sky.

"We need protection from predators!"

"Yeah!" Deth and Tacks yelled.

"It's time for someone to take care of us!" Wug shouted.

This time scattered applause.

"A higher power should guide our prey to us!"

"Woo-hoo!" People were getting into it now.

"So we don't have to hunt far and wide!"

Now there was a burst of clapping

"Leaving our families vulnerable!" Wug shouted.

This struck a chord and the cave people stood in a rush, cheering wildly.

Wug waited for the audience's pause to catch their breath and, timing it perfectly, shouted in his great big voice…

_"WE. NEED. A. GOD!"

The place went nuts.

Deth and Tacks were beating on each other. The entire tribe was cheering, clapping, whooping and dancing. Even dour Droog was standing, smiling and clapping.

Area Wug and Berp stood there, arms crossed, basking in the celebration with triumphant smiles spread across their faces. They studiously ignored a deep rumble from the skies. A fat raindrop splattered onto the log next to them.

Finally the village's collective celebratory spasm petered out, and there was a shuffling sound as everyone took their seats again.

When everyone was settled, Wug raised his arms again, and the crowd quieted.

"Okay, is everyone ready?" he asked.

They were a bit worn emotionally, but there were smiles and nods all around.

"Then it's time."

"Time for what?" Droog asked.

Wug grinned, "We are going to create our god. Right here, right now."

Deth looked around, "What are we going to make him out of? These logs?"

"No, silly," Wug said. "We're going to create Him, by the power of …"

"What do you mean, 'Him'?" Hedz interrupted, forgetting she wasn't supposed to speak in Council.

"Yeah," Yerba chimed. "How do you know God is a Him?"

"And if we're creating Her, we can just choose," Hedz said.

Wug's mouth was open, so Berp replied, "Of course God is a guy. How can He protect us from predators if He's a She?"

"Actually, if He's cute, I don't mind a guy," Sheez said demurely.

There was silence as the cave guys paused to look at Sheez and soak in the sight of her newfound chest ravine.

Wug finally found his voice, "Of course God's a He …"

"We could have two gods," Hedz interrupted. "A She and a He."

"You mean, 'He and She,'" Berp said, who had also forgotten women were prohibited from speaking in Council.

Hedz didn't even spare him a glance. "And maybe they could have baby gods."

"A baby god would be so cute," Gop gushed.

Wug was waving his arm up and down, slamming nothing onto nothing.

Bonk noticed and said helpfully, "We haven't invented a hammer and gavel yet."

Wug looked startled, but stopped waving his arm.

"God is a man," he growled.

Hedz finally took pity on him, "Fine, our first god can be a guy, but the next one has to be a woman."

"Made from the guy's ribs," Deth blurted.

There was a silence as everyone looked at him.

He held his palms up, "What?"

"That's kinda grotesque," Gop said.

"Okay," Hedz said. "Now that that's settled, how do we go about creating our God?"

Sensing control of the meeting drifting back in his general direction, Area Wug grabbed it. "We pray."

Suddenly Lob popped up behind Wug, whispered in his ear, and shoved a dead raccoon in Wug's hand. Then the small caveman disappeared like a hairy leprechaun.

Surreptitiously stroking the raccoon's pelt, Wug added, "And there will be prayer in school."

"What's school?" Bonk asked.

"Um, it's, uh, school. You know. Like school," Wug said helplessly.

Lob popped back up and whispered again. Then he was gone.

Wug straightened up, "Schools are where the kids learn things."

"Like what?" Droog asked.

"Like, um, like ..." Wug's face clouded over. "Look, we'll get back to the school thing later. Let's get back to the praying thing." He leaned towards the on-looking crowd, seeking each caveperson's eyes. "Prayer is when you wish really hard for something."

"I wish the girls would stand up so we can see them better," Tacks said.

Wug shot him a glare. "No, not stuff like that. We have to reach deep inside us…"

"Is this that rib thing again?" Gop asked.

"No, no. You…" Wug took a deep breath, composing himself. "Prayer is when you believe in something…"

"I believe it's going to rain," Deth said, pointing to the sky, which was starting to look just about as angry as Wug.

Wug ground his teeth together and hissed through clenched jaws," We wish for something with every ounce of …"

"What's an ounce?" someone shouted.

One of Wug's molars chipped but he soldiered on, "..our souls…"

"What's a soul?" someone else shouted.

"STOP IT!" Wug screamed.

There was silence, punctuated by another low rumbling of thunder.

Wug looked as if he might soon suffer the very first heart attack.

"I think I know what he's saying," Hedz said, taking pity on the chief. "But a god is something we have to believe in before prayer works. But the problem is you can't pray for a god without the god already existing. So we have to first believe, and only then will prayer work."

Wug chewed that thought for a moment, swallowed it and then, eyes blazing, snarled, "Well, I do believe in a God. He's a he …"

He shot a defiant look at Hedz, who just shrugged. Then he continued, "And He will watch over us. He will make us better swimmers, He will make us better hunters. He will bring fertility. He will have strange powers of defense. He will protect us from predators."

Wug looked out over the assembled cave people, and thundered. "Will you believe in Him with me? Will you help me bring Him here to watch over us? To make our lives easier? Will you BELIEVE!"

The villagers surged to their feet and erupted, "YES! WE BELIEVE!"

"I BELIEVE!" Wug shouted.

"WE BELIEVE!" they shouted back.

"WE BELIEVE!" Wug and the crowd shouted in unison.

A thunderous boom suddenly crashed down from the heavens and a bolt of lightning seared the sky, strobing their little slice of earth in an instant of light and earsplitting noise. Women screamed, men shouted in alarm, children and babies cried. And in that instant of illumination an eagle flew low over the ridge, its head devoid of feathers, clutching something in its claws. The bolt flashed the eagle, causing it to lose its grip on the struggling form. The object tumbled to the ground, landing at Wug's feet. The eagle screeched indignantly, and winged away.

And as the bald eagle flapped away over the trees, the cave people saluted.

"Why are we saluting?" Droog hissed at Bonk from the cover of his mouth.

"I don't know," Bonk hissed back.

In moments, the majestic eagle was gone, and the cave people looked at the small object heaven's winged messenger had deposited at their leader's feet.

Drogg scratched himself and looked critically at the platypus. "I guess when we prayed for a god, we should have specified we wanted one in our image."

Then the downpour hit.

Chapter 28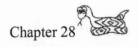

The next morning brought sun and warmth. Frigg and Bush had burped out of the cave early, and were sauntering down the path just being boys and looking for something to relieve the boredom. They'd left early to avoid Hedz who might just assign them some work that would relieve the boredom, but at the expense of fun. Neither of them felt like hunting or foraging, so when Hedz wasn't looking they'd bolted out of the cave.

As they strolled down the path, keeping an alert eye out for cave bears and dire wolves, they picked up rocks, tossing them in the river meandering along the path. "Can't wait until we invent baseball," Bush said, just missing a heron with a curve ball.

"Yeah, or football," Frigg agreed. "Hey, you know we have to …"

Suddenly, something slithered across the path.

"Aaagh, an attorney," Frigg shrieked. He shot up into the air like a startled mongoose.

"Jorj!" Bush cried.

Frigg shot him a jealous glance. "Jorj it all anyway, I forgot to use our new cussword."

"You have to stay on top of things like that if you want to manufacture a bad habit." Bush was pleased he'd remembered while his older brother hadn't.

"Yeah, but it's a false alarm," Frigg said. He pointed at the slimy creature. "It's not an attorney."

Bush looked closely. Yes, it was a reptile, but indeed was not an attorney,

"See, it's just a snake," Frigg said.

"Yeah, okay. That thing nearly scared me out of my boxers," Bush said.

"Is that what you call those?" Frigg said, cutting eyes at Bush's outfit.

Bush was wearing furs tied around his genital and gluteus, but pulled down in back, exposing several inches of butt crack.

"Yeah, you like'em?" Bush asked.

"I don't know. What's the deal with the butt crack?"

Bush looked back at his own personal ravine and grinned, "I wear them really low as a fashion sense. Pretty cool, huh?"

"I dunno. They're hanging all the way down to your knees. You can't run with them like that. What if we run into the sloth or something?"

"I just rip them off. Or I use them to fight," Bush said.

Frigg's bushy eyebrows jumped, "You're going to fight with boxers?"

"Well, not exactly. Look." Bush reached his hand deep into the crack and pulled out a short sharp stick. "See, I can keep stuff there, like this."

"A baby spear?" Frigg asked.

"No, I call it a knife," Bush said. "You can slash and defend yourself with it."

Frigg looked at the little stick. "I don't know. If we ran into a predator, I'd want a bigger stick than that."

Bush didn't answer, his attention on the snake wriggling across the path. "Here, watch."

Frigg's eyes went wide, "Hey, it might be poisonous!"

"Don't worry," Bush replied. He jogged after the snake who, quickly realizing it couldn't outrun the cave boy, stopped and coiled, raising its head and hissing a warning.

Bush ignored the threat, sidestepped the snake's lunge, and stabbed it in the middle of the back. The snake went rigid as the stick severed the nerve endings that connected brain and muscles. That's okay though, because there was no such thing as the ASPCA yet to protect its rights.

Bush pointed at the snake, which for some reason hadn't gone into death throes. "See, I killed a dangerous serpent with it."

"It's not dead," noted Frigg.

Bush lifted the impaled snake to eye level. It looked back unblinkingly and flicked its tongue. It clearly was still alive. "Huh, weird." He shrugged, "Well, I always wanted a pet."

Frigg chuckled. That was the truth. "Remember when you tried to domesticate the wolf?"

Bush nodded. "Yeah, that was a mistake. I still have marks from that one." He shuddered. "No one's ever going to be able to domesticate a wolf."

"And the baby saber-tooth?" Frigg said.

Bush grimaced. "Yeah, another catastrophe. Okay, I admit my efforts to get a pet haven't been very successful. But this…" he gestured to the immobile snake, "… might be a different story. It can't bite me, it can't run away."

"Crawl," Frigg said dryly.

"Or crawl," Bush said. "Yep, this is the perfect pet."

"Maybe," Frigg said. "But what can it do?"

Bush and the snake looked at each other. The snake was purple with yellow markings.

Then Bush took a rock and tossed it. "Fetch!" he cried. The snake didn't twitch.

"Speak," Bush commanded.

The snake flicked a tongue out, but remained silent.

"Roll over."

The snake was impaled to a stick, but didn't bother to mention this detail to his owner.

"Hmmm, I don't know. Maybe just use him to scare girls," Bush said.

Frigg shook his head. "Maybe. Some of the girls I know are more likely to scare a snake than the other way around."

"Yeah, you might be right. I'll figure something out."

"You always do," Frigg grinned.

Bush nodded in agreement with himself. "I just have to find a better way to carry him around. Don't I, little guy?" he cooed to the snake.

The snake just looked at him.

Bush went into the trees lining the river and snapped off a four-foot sapling right above a branch. Next he yanked a thin vine from around a tree trunk, and careful to keep away from the snake's fangs, he lashed the snake to the top of the stick, so that its body was tied securely to the stick with its head resting on the crook of the branch.

"This is so Sssss can watch where we're going," Bush said.

"Sssss?"

"Yeah, another component about pets is you have to name them."

Frigg shook his head. "I dunno. I have a feeling that when you bring it home, we're going to end up eating it."

Bush's eyes went wide, "People don't eat pets!"

"Nobody has pets."

"I don't care," Bush said. "We're not eating Sssss, and that's it."

Frigg just shrugged, and started back down the path. Bush hesitated and then started after his brother.

When he caught up, Frigg said, "You know. We need to create a lewd gesture."

"Huh?" Bush said, his attention on the snake lashed onto his walking stick.

Frigg looked both ways before continuing. "A gesture. Like we can call someone a Jorj, but what if we want to demonstrate our contempt without audibling?"

This time Bush looked up, "What the Jorj are you talking about?"

"Jorj works pretty good for a verbal insult. Or you can call them a 'knuckle-dragger."

Bush straightened up. He occasionally put a knuckle down to help with his balance.

"Think about it," Frigg said, waving his arms. "What do you do if you want to insult someone but for some reason you can't say anything out loud?"

"Throw poop at them?"

"Well, yes, you can do that. But what if throwing poop isn't practical for some reason?"

"How about a rock then?"

"Same thing."

Bush's face was a mask of confusion. "I guess I don't know,"

"A gesture. You gesture at them with something that would insult them."

"Okay, how about this?" Bush asked. He wheeled around and farted.

"Yeah, that's definitely nasty," Frigg acknowledged. "But it won't work for long range insults."

"How about this?" Bush said, holding up his fist with the middle finger extended.

Frigg frowned. "I don't get it."

Bush looked at the finger. "Yeah, stupid. Flipping this at someone will never catch on."

Frigg paused, and tossed another rock in the river. "We'll just stick that on the back burner for now."

"The what?"

"The back burner."

"What's that mean?" Bush asked.

"Um, nothing yet. But it will some day."

Bush just shook his head. Sometimes Frigg said things just to confuse him, and it was better to just nod and move on. Then he saw something.

"Who's that?" he said, pointing at a humanoid shape lying by the side of the path.

"Not who. I think it's a what," Frigg said.

They crept closer to the body.

"Is it alive?" Bush asked.

"I dunno," Frigg said, pausing a few feet away.

Bush stuck the snake stick out, prodding the hairy body with the snake's head. The snake's tongue flicked over the figure which didn't move.

"That proves it's dead," Bush concluded. "No one alive would let a snake lick it."

"Yeah, I think you're right," Frigg said, edging closer.

"So what is it?" Bush asked.

Frigg shrugged. "Looks like some kind of monkey."

"What happened to it?"

Frigg turned the body over. It was still a bit warm, but definitely dead. He looked around. There was a broken branch lying nearby. Frigg looked up at a nearby tree and saw a fresh break near the top.

"I think it fell from there," he said, pointing at the break.

Bush looked up, assessed the distance, and nodded. "Yep, that would do it," he agreed. He looked down at the monkey. There was a fair amount of meat on the body. "What do we do with it?"

Frigg had been wondering the same thing. "I dunno. I can't figure out if we should eat it or bury it. It's hard to tell if we're far enough removed genetically to rationalize eating it."

"Yeah, we could be distantly related," Bush said.

"It does look like Uncle Gerf," Frigg said, grinning.

Bush poked it with the snake, "What do you think, snake?" The snake licked its lips.

"Okay, we eat it," Bush decided. If they brought home meat, Hedz would be less likely to insist on them eating his snake.

Frigg shrugged. He'd come to the same conclusion. He knew better than to take a gift monkey for granted.

Chapter 29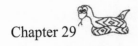

Bonk was sitting outside the cave, watching the day disk rush towards the clouds that were hauling in the afternoon showers. It was a bit too bright for him to look at for long. He was starting to seriously wonder if the day disk was the source of heat when it was light. Or even more, the source of the light. He wondered if he were walk far away whether the disk would follow. He resolved to make the attempt some day. Maybe when the kids were a little older.

There was a light sandy thump as someone slid to a seat next to him. Hedz, looking mighty fine in her furs and mustaches.

"Hey," Bonk said.

"Hey, yourself." She looked up where he had been looking, and shaded her eyes. "What's up?"

"It's the disk," he said, giving it a glance. "I'm just wondering about it."

"Hmmm."

"Like it's usually warm down here when it's up there," he said.

"Hmmm," she responded.

He gave her a glance but she didn't appear to be making fun of him. "But it flies over when there's snow on the ground, too."

"Hmmm."

"But there are times when both the day disk and the night disk come out." Bonk frowned. "Is it possible the light disk brings the light? And the night disk brings the dark?"

Hedz hugged her knees. "Sometimes you can see both at the same time."

Bonk mulled it over. She was right.

"I wonder if I could follow it someday," he said hopefully. "See where it goes."

"Maybe, someday," she said noncommittally.

Bonk thought carefully. "If the day disk brings heat, maybe there's some way we could capture it and use it for warmth."

"I think it might be a bit higher than you think," Hedz said.

"Yeah, I know it's higher than the trees, and it goes over the mountain range." He shrugged. "But how high can it be?"

Hedz didn't answer.

"And the night disk. Sometimes it's only partially there."

"Sometimes it's not there at all," Hedz pointed out.

He nodded.

"Hey, remember my wheel?" Once again, he ignored the slight flash of irritation over having been scammed out of it.

"Yes."

"It's shaped like that. I wonder if it rolls across the sky, or if it just slides."

She shrugged, taking pleasure in his pensive mood.

"But clouds defeat them both," Bonk said. "So clouds must be the strongest force."

"I think clouds are made of water," Hedz said. "And when bits break off, they fall on us."

He thought about it.

"I wish we would get around to inventing counting and numbers," he said after a moment.

She turned and looked at him. "Counting?"

"And a calendar, that'd be cool, too. Then we could keep track on when the night disk comes. And other stuff, too. I mean, heck, we haven't invented weekends yet. We need a weekend."

135

"Why?"

"How else can we know when we can rest?"

"We're resting right now," she pointed out.

"Well, yes. But we don't get that many opportunities. And I'm feeling guilty about it because I'm not hunting right now."

"Maybe, but this is nice for right now." Hedz shifted so their shoulders touched. This was the first time Hedz had allowed contact since the vote for female rights. She had, well, withdrawn certain privileges.

"Are we okay now?" he asked, boldly stepping onto that ice.

She arched a huge furry brow, "What do you mean?"

"Um, well, you know, I know you weren't happy…" he stammered.

"Are you talking about the vote?" she asked.

"Uh. Maybe."

She snuggled closer, "Don't worry about that. We don't need to vote. You'll simply do what I say, right?"

"Uh, yeah?"

"Same as it ever was. You guys can have your guy meetings, vote on stuff, as long as you know …" She looked deeply into his eyes, " … really know .. who's actually in charge."

"Right," he said, his insides sliding around in a weird way.

Hedz looked back at the sky. "I've been wondering about the disks, too. I think the day disk is fire and the night disk is ice. But lightning is the one I can't figure out. It comes when the day and night disks have been driven away by the clouds. Yet somehow it brings fire down to us. How can that be?"

Bonk thought about it. "Can clouds somehow take fire from the day disk?"

"I don't know. It is weird that the clouds bring water and then they bring lightning that brings fire. How can they bring both water and fire?"

Bonk nodded, remembering how the water immediately quenched his flame.

"I don't know," Hedz replied. "Even more weird, lightning is the same color as the night disk, which I think is made of ice. But once it creates fire, the fire is the color of the day disk. I don't understand."

"Definitely weird," Bonk agreed.

Hedz sighed. "I don't know if we will ever discover the answers, unless we learn to fly or something."

Bonk snorted a snot bubble.

"Who knows?" Hedz grinned. "Maybe we'll sprout feathers. Evolve or something."

"Evolution?" Bonk laughed. "Ridiculous."

"Yeah, like we'll get bigger and smarter," Hedz said.

"Well, I hope animals get smaller," Bonk said. These crocs and sloths are just too darn big."

"In the meantime," Hedz continued, "we need that fire."

"Yeah, fire was nice and warm," Bonk agreed.

Hedz pointed at the storm clouds collecting on the horizon. "So when the clouds get here and bring us fire, you have to catch it."

"Don't you mean we?" Bonk asked.

She patted his arm, "No, honey, you are the Fire God, remember?"

"Oh, yeah. Heh, heh," he said nervously.

He wasn't a big fan of thunder.

Chapter 30

"The Meefs are arming themselves," Lob whispered in Wug's ear.

Wug jumped, and whirled, "Jeepers, would you please make some noise when you sneak up on me!"

Lob frowned, "If I made noise, it wouldn't be sneaking."

"Fine, then don't sneak up on me at all. Stomp when you're coming at me."

"Yessir," Lob said. "Sorry about that. Here, accept this as my apology."

He slid a couple catfish into Wug's hands. Wug's hands moved by themselves to take possession of the food. It seemed the more Lob gave him stuff, the more readily Wug's hands moved to accept the gifts.

"What was it you said about the Meefs?" Wug asked, sneaking a glance at the catfish. They were plump, well fed and still alive, gills flapping as they gasped for water. Wug's mouth watered.

"I saw them," Lob said. "I snuck up on their camp and saw them preparing advanced weaponry."

"You're definitely good at sneaking," Wug agreed.

"Yes. And they are making many, many spears. I think they are planning on attacking us."

Wug's eyebrows furrowed. "Why would they attack us?"

"Why to get our fine caves, of course," Lob replied.

Wug didn't even know where Lob lived.

"I thought they lived in trees," Wug said. "Why would they want to live in a hole in the ground?"

138

"They probably just want your women," Lob said.

"What?! No way. They can't have our women!"

"There's only one thing you can do," Lob said. "You need to start building your own armies."

Another peculiar phrase.

"What are armies?" Wug asked.

"Armies are groups of your people armed with weapons," Lob said. "Hence, arms…armies."

"Oh, so if we fought with our legs, we'd be leggies?" Wug joshed.

Lob just looked at him with his watery eyes.

"Ah, er, anyway. What is a weapon?"

"A weapon is a tool that is used to hurt someone," Lob said.

"Oh, like duct tape?" Wug asked.

Lob felt a surge of contempt, but easily hid it, "No, like spears. It's a tool when hunting, but a weapon when used for defense or for battling other humans."

Wug thought about it, and a sick feeling went through him at the thought of fighting other humans.

Lob must have sensed it because he went on. "Fortunately, the Meefs are not really humans. They are, rather, a subspecies. No better than animals themselves."

"So it's okay to kill them?" Wug asked.

Lob nodded. "Yes, definitely."

"Can we eat them?"

Lob looked uncomfortable, "Well, I doubt if you'd want to. I heard they don't taste good."

Chapter 31

There was a low rumbling and Area Wug looked up to see how far away the storm was. When he looked back at Lob, the little caveman was gone, as quickly and quietly as he had appeared. It was almost as if he was an illusion. Wug looked down, and saw he still had the catfish. So Lob must have been real. Weird.

He shrugged off the feeling. It was time to worship the new god.

Outside the cave was a small ledge where Wug had placed the platypus god. The ledge had a sharp drop-off and there was no easy way for the small platypus to scramble off. And since it was a god, Wug figured if it really wanted to leave, it could.

"What's up, boss," came a voice behind him.

"Crap!" Wug shrieked and whirled around. "I wish people would stop sneaking up on me!"

"Sorry," Berp said, not really looking sorry at all. "So how's God doing?"

"I don't know. I was just going to check," Wug replied.

They walked to the other side of the cave's mouth and looked over at a small rock outcropping that was just a few feet over. A bird had once built a nest on there, but the bird was long gone, mostly because Wug had eaten both the bird and its eggs. The nest didn't taste as good, so he had left it. It proved to be a convenient place to keep a god.

Somewhat to his surprise, the platypus was still there. An excellent indication that it accepted its God-hood role. They looked at the platypus. The platypus looked back at them with beady eyes. It didn't look like a god, but seeing as they didn't know what a god was supposed to look like, they guessed it was as godlike as anything else.

"So you're a god." Wug murmured.

Berp's face was expectant, like he might see the platypus sprout wings or something. He lowered himself to his knees.

"What are you doing?" Wug asked.

"You're supposed to be on your knees when you talk with gods."

"Oh." Wug knelt.

The two cavemen looked up at the platypus which was sniffing around the nest, pushing aside twigs with its wide bill.

"Now what?" Wug asked, sliding a look over to Berp.

"I think we just ask it for stuff," Berp replied.

"Yeah, that makes sense," Wug said. He raised his eyes back to the platypus. "Dear God. Please bring us food."

Just then, one of the catfish Lob had brought gave a last twitch. Berp looked down and his eyes went wide. He grabbed a fish and scrambled to his feet. "Hey, it worked! Look, God brought us food."

Wug was still kneeling. "Uh, well, not exactly…"

"What are you talking about? We asked God for food, and then these catfish just appeared. You think they swam here? Nope, God brought them." Berp started dancing. "Woo-hoo! God is good! God is mighty!"

Wug started to explain where the catfish had come from, but to be honest, he was still having trouble understanding Lob. Where had the little caveman come from? What were the secrets to his appearances and disappearances? Maybe Lob had been brought there by the god. So maybe Berp was right after all.

Slowly, Wug raised his massive bulk from his knees, and a broad grin grew across his face. "Yes, God provided. Just as we knew He would. Our faith is justified."

141

The platypus nuzzled the nest, knocking branches off the ledge.

"Look, I think the God is hungry," Berp said. "We must feed Him."

"Yes, we must sacrifice some of our food," Wug agreed. He bit a piece off one of the catfish, and held it out to the platypus. The creature gave the fish a cautious sniff, and then snatched the offering.

"It accepted our sacrifice," Berp shouted, doing a little jig. "God accepts us!"

"Yes, God is great," Wug said.

Chapter 32

Dork was strolling down the river looking for large stones for his henge, and spied Yerba, a village cavewoman, kneeling on the sandy bank next to a huge mound of sand. He couldn't tell what she was doing.

Being naturally curious, Dork detoured over and headed for the riverbank. Just before he reached Yerba, a leaf blew against his leg. He was going to kick it off, but then noticed something strange about it. He reached down and examined its black markings. He rubbed the markings and they smudged. The chalky-like substance was the same as what was left from his burned Woodhenge. Shrugging, he dropped the leaf, and it went bouncing along the bank.

Now he could see Yerba had captured a small river creature and was using a sharp stone to peel the fur away from fat and muscle.

"What's up, Yerba?" he asked.

She paused, and looked up. "Making a purse."

He frowned. "A purse?"

"Yes, something I can keep stuff in," she said, resuming the task.

"Hmmm, interesting," Dork said. "Stuff like what?"

She shrugged. "You know, cosmetics, soft tissuey leaves and other female stuff."

Female stuff, huh? Hmm, better not to go there.

Before he could say anything else, she looked up again. "Do you know what that is?" she asked, gesturing to the large pile of sand.

143

He colored. It was the remnants of Sandhenge, his first attempt at making a henge. It hadn't held up past the first rainstorm.

"Um, no, no, I don't," he stammered, hoping she wouldn't notice his blushing.

She wasn't watching anyway, and kept slicing.

When Dork saw how easily the sharp stone cut through muscle and fat, an idea came to him. "Where did you get that stone?" he asked.

"Over by the landslide," she said, pointing to where a large part of a cliff had collapsed some time ago, wiping out a small family of cave rabbits.

"Ah, okay, thank you. Good luck with your purse," he said, stepping over what was left of Sandhenge and heading off towards the landslide.

"No problem," Yerba replied, intent on her task.

Chapter 33

Hedz was feeding Eff at the cave mouth when Bonk came out, spear in hand.

Back then, cave guys didn't know they were supposed to tell their mate where they were going and when they would come back, which was pretty unfair considering the concept of 'when' was still pretty much theoretical.

"Where do you think you're going, Buster?" Hedz said. "You're supposed to stay here and watch for fire tonight." She gestured at the rapidly approaching rainclouds.

"I will. I mean, I'm going to. But if I'm going to run around in a thunderstorm in the middle of plains filled with all manner of lions and rhinos, I'm going to need protection."

"You have your spear. What else do you need?"

Bonk just looked at her.

Hedz grimaced. Bonk knew exactly what Hedz thought of his expertise with a spear.

She relented. "Okay." Then curiosity struck, "What kind of protection?"

"I'm going to go see Hrmph and see if he can whip up a defensive charm."

Hrmph was the local shaman.

Hedz's eyes went wide. "What, that old charlatan? He couldn't protect you from the common cold. If we got decent medical around here, we could get rid of the common cold forever."

Bonk shook his head, "I don't know, the common cold is a survivor."

145

Hedz snorted, "Hah, as soon as we get competent medical facilities, the common cold will be as extinct as those big old giant animals who left their bones all over the place."

"Yeah, maybe. But what would it hurt if I just had a charm anyway, just for luck?"

Hedz shooed him away, "Fine, go get your good luck charm... for whatever good it does. But have him make his lucky charms edible, so if they don't work, we can eat them. Oh, and get back here by the time the lightning show starts."

The Shaman's cave was located in the most downwind of caves. The biggest reason for its location was because Hrmph's cave was filled with bits and parts of deceased animals Hrmph had either found after the scavengers were done with them, or scrounged from the piles of trash at the foot of the villager's caves where they were simply tossed after consumption. The trash contained all kinds of wonderful things, like the jawbone of asses, anuses from all manner of beasts (they were too chewy, so generally discarded, though some people used them as the first chewing gum). There were also ripped up ears, feathers, cracked bones, claws, globules of inedible meat and other treasures a witch doctor used to whip together potions and other spells. The trouble was after sitting in a cave too long, the pungent smell was enough to offend cavemen. Which said something, since cavemen generally could tolerate some pretty bad smells.

Bonk climbed the steep incline to the Shaman's cave, wrinkling his nose against the odors that increased as he got closer. The last few steps were the worst, and his eyes were watering by the time he got to the cave's mouth.

There was no one there.

"Hello?" Bonk asked, holding his nose and peering into the gloom of the cave.

His voice echoed, but no one answered.

"Hellooooo?" he repeated.

Still nothing.

"Looking for me?"

The voice came from above the cave. Bonk looked up, and saw the old witchdoctor sitting on the hill above the cave.

"Yeah. Just a sec." Skirting the cave, Bonk climbed the rest of the way to where Hrmph was sitting with a large leaf on his lap.

"You want a baby mouse?" Hrmph picked up the leaf and shoved it towards Bonk. On the leaf were several little pink wriggling shapes.

"Um, no thanks, I already ate," Bonk said.

"Suit yourself," Hrmph said, picking up a mouse nugget and popping it in his mouth.

"What are you doing up here?" Bonk asked, looking for any sign that the doctor was performing some kind of experiment on the side of the hill.

"Ah, that," Hrmph said. "Got a bit of a small situation. Some weasel kidneys went bad."

"Really? I hadn't noticed," Bonk lied.

Hrmph shot Bonk a dubious squint. "So what can I do for you, Bonk?"

Now Bonk's idea was seeming a bit far fetched. Catch fire? Ridiculous.

"Well, I've got to go on a dangerous journey and I need a protective charm," he said, dancing around the truth.

Hrmph popped another mouse in his mouth, releasing a small foul cloud of bad breath. "Protective charm, eh? There are many different charms available for that. What do you need protection from?"

Bonk shuffled his feet, "Well, lions ... and woolly rhinos ... "

"Those are easy enough," Hrmph said.

"... and fire."

Hrmph stopped chewing. "Fire?"

147

"Yes, the yellow hot stuff that…"

"I know what fire is," Hrmph snapped. He frowned, considering. "Hmmm, fire, huh? That's not going to be easy. It's going to cost you a pretty penny."

"Penny?"

Hrmph waved his hand, "Just a figure of speech. Do you have insurance for this kind of thing?"

"Insurance, what's that?"

"It's something that you buy hoping you'll never have to use it," Hrmph said.

"Why would I want to buy something not to use?" Bonk asked, a vision of his swindled wheel flashing in his mind. He shook the thought off.

Hrmph shook his hand, "Never mind. I'll just sell the charm to you outright. Do you have any money?"

"Money?"

"Goods, something you can trade me."

"Um."

Bonk looked down at himself. He was naked. All he had was his spear, and a not so very good spear at that. He had nothing of value.

"Hey!"

Bonk looked down the hill. His sons Frigg and Bush were climbing the hill. It looked like Frigg was dragging a hairy kid and Bush had a walking stick with two eyes on the end. As he looked, he could have sworn the stick flicked out a forked tongue.

"Hi, boys, what'cha got there?" Bonk asked.

Frigg looked up and grinned, "We got dinner."

As they got closer, Bonk could see that it was a monkey, rather than a hairy kid, which was a common mistake, seeing that the cave people were rather hairy. Still, though, the monkey's face looked kind of familiar.

"It looks like Uncle Gerf, doesn't it?" Bush asked.

148

Bonk cocked his head. Sonuvagun, it did look a bit like his long lost brother. Lost because the last time the tribe had gone nomadic, Gerf had disappeared into some bushes for a potty break, and when he came out, the tribe had moved on. Gerf had yet to catch up.

"It's not him though," Frigg said. "It's definitely a monkey."

"Do you guys really think we should eat monkey?" Bonk asked. "Seems almost cannibalistic."

"We were wondering about that, too. We decided just to bring it home and let the parental units take that decision out of our hands," Frigg said.

"I'd eat it," Bush declared.

Bonk started to say something and then he noticed the snake strapped onto Bush's walking stick. He pointed. "Um, isn't that…?"

Bush grinned. "Yep, meet Sssss." He brandished the stick. The snake got a vaguely nauseated look as it was rattled around.

"Sssss?"

"Yep, a snake. I killed it with my knife."

"Knife?" Bonk asked.

"Baby spear, don't ask," Frigg responded before Bush could give another demonstration of the stick's ability.

Hrmph was watching with interest. Finally, he said, "I could take that monkey off your hands."

Frigg hugged the monkey's arm, "My monkey."

"If you give it to me, I'd be willing to make the charm Bonk was negotiating for," the medicine man said. "Seems he's bit short on funds right now. Give me the monkey, and we'll call it even."

Frigg looked doubtfully at Bonk, who shrugged.

Hrmph had an eager look on his face. "You wanted fire. Seems like a mighty fine tradeoff for a dead critter."

149

"Hedz sent me out for fire," Bonk explained to the boys. "But I figured on getting Hrmph's blessing before I run out into the rain and fire and predators and all that."

"So you want me to give up the monkey?" Frigg asked.

"No! We can't. Hedz will eat my snake," Bush cried, hugging the stick. The snake licked his shoulder.

"Give him the monkey. I'll make sure … is that snake alive?!" Bonk shrieked.

"Well, yeah. When I killed him he didn't exactly die. So now it's my pet." Bush cradled the stick to his chest. The snake just looked at Bonk.

Bonk thought quickly. Hedz hadn't sent him after food. She'd told him to catch fire. The Shaman would create a charm that would help him get the fire. So if they gave the monkey to Hrmph, it would, in essence be what Hedz wanted.

"Um, you haven't exactly had success with pets," Bonk pointed out.

"Yeah, I know. The wolf and cat. But this guy is the bomb," Bush said, giving the snake a fond look. The snake pooped.

"Fine, if you give him the monkey I'll make sure we don't eat the snake." Bonk looked at the snake again. It was lashed to the walking stick. A smaller stick was sticking like a stick from the snake's back. "How do you plan on feeding it?"

"I've been giving it crickets. It seems to like them fine," Bush said.

Bonk nodded slowly. There was a small bulge in the middle of the snake's body. "Okay, we won't eat it, unless it dies on its own. Then all bets are off."

Bush frowned. "Bets?"

Bonk waved it off, "It's just an expression. Except I'm the first to ever say it."

Bush just looked confused, "Well, okay."

Frigg dragged the monkey over to the Shaman. "Here you go, old man. Do your thing."

Chapter 34

The closer Dork got to the landslide, the more difficult the footing. Bits of rock and stone had been strewn about haphazardly. When the lip of the hill collapsed, it had brought down the entire cliff face. Some of the rock shards had broken into sheets that lay scattered over the field. He picked up one of the smaller rocks and to his surprised delight, the sharp edge cut deeply into his thumb callus.

He grinned, and stepped around a large pile of rocks, nearly tripping over another caveman.

Well, not exactly another caveman. It was Steve, one of the oddest members of the village. You also couldn't really call him a caveman because of a severe case of claustrophobia which kept him out of caves. He lived, instead, in a hut made out of sticks.

Physically, he was a freak with a light complexion and an overlarge head. He had narrow shoulders, wide hips, and because his arms were freakishly short, barely hanging down to his knees, he was unable to drop to all fours and run. As if these deformities weren't enough, his hair was nearly white, with a large round patch on the top of his bulbous head where no hair grew. The skin was pink, shiny and usually sun-burnt.

These unfortunate calamities of birth combined to make him a horrible hunter, so he eked out a living gathering what grubs he could find under rocks and fallen logs. Then he'd go back to his hut and sit for hours, munching fatty grubs, watching cockroaches pooping and fighting over scraps on the rocks around his hut. He called this cockroach-watching hobby,

'Reality TV.' None of the other cavemen knew or cared what he was talking about.

His sedentary lifestyle and rich foods led to a pronounced gut, something no other caveman had achieved. Sometimes a woman might develop a similar rounded tummy, but each case eventually led to a new cave baby. As of yet, Steve's rounded belly had yet to yield an infant, but the tribe kept a curious eye on the situation anyway. In the meantime, he was friendly enough, so the other cavemen let him hang around rather than chasing him away.

Steve was sitting on his haunches, bent over something. As Dork approached, the misshapen caveman looked over his shoulder and shifted to hide what he was working on.

"What do you want," Steve hissed, blue eyes narrowed. He was the only caveman in the village without brown eyes.

Dork pulled up, shocked by his attitude. "Oh, sorry. I didn't see you." He tried to see what Steve was hiding. It wasn't like cavemen to be secretive.

Steve turned away a bit more. "Nothing. It's mine. You can't have it."

Dork's eyebrows shot up. Then, because they were heavy, gravity overcame his forehead muscles and the eyebrows dropped back where they belonged. "Don't worry. I'm not going to take anything from you."

Steve just growled, showing soft nubby teeth. Dork felt a flash of pity at the display of inadequate incisors. No wonder he didn't eat much meat.

There was a brief rumble from the sky and they both looked up. The storm was getting closer.

Dork dropped down in a squat, "C'mon, man. You've known me all your life. I'd never do anything to you."

Steve considered this, and after a moment concluded that Dork was a stand up guy. He had never been one to pick on him, torment or bully him.

"Okay," he said, reluctantly showing what he had been working on.

Dork gasped. It was a spear. But not a normal spear. Steve had taken a sharp stone and fitted it into the split end of the spear. Then he had lashed it tight with some kind of stringy animal gut. The rock was nicely chipped into a shape that fit perfectly into the groove, complete with knobby protrusions positioned to keep the rock anchored to the spear.

Dork had to admire the craftsmanship. "Amazing. That's just superb. I was thinking something like this was possible. In fact, that's why I came out here."

Steve snatched the spear to his chest. "It's mine. I invented it. It's patented."

Dork frowned, "Patent?"

"Yeah. That means no one else can make it without paying me." Steve displayed his teeth again.

"Okay, okay," Dork said, barely managing to hide a smile. Steve's dentistry wouldn't scare a cave mouse.

*

Chapter 35

"This is pretty cool," Frigg said, looking at the small tangled pile of twigs twisty-tied with a myriad array of unidentifiable plant and body parts.

After taking possession of the monkey, the Shaman had retreated back to his cave and come back some time later with a pungent charm he guaranteed to keep them safe. Of course, if it didn't, Bonk would be dead, so he'd hardly be in a position to demand a refund. As a bonus, Hrmph had given them another charm he claimed would keep them dry. But he'd cautioned them that the effect wouldn't last long and it might have side effects that might make it dangerous. His warning had sufficiently scared them, and Bonk had decreed they would only use it if they needed it.

Now Bonk, Frigg and Bush were hurrying along the path, trying to beat the oncoming thunderstorm.

They climbed the hill home where they found a line of young cavemen snaking into the cave.

"What the...?" Bonk said, climbing past them. The cavemen shot him the resentful looks that all humans in line use when someone tries to cut in front of them. Frigg and Bush ignored them and ducked into the cave.

Hedz was sitting at the mouth of the cave, watching the roiling black clouds overhead. Behind her, Eff was splayed out on the huge dinosaur bone trying to eat her own fist.

"Who are all of these people?" Bonk asked, gesturing to the young men.

"Gop's interviewing potential mates," Hedz said.

155

Bonk surveyed the cavemen in line. Most of them were in that range just between child and man. "Is she still planning on starting a harem?"

"Probably. She doesn't think a single man could handle her."

Bonk nodded. That was probably true.

"By the way, she said you left the seed up on the latrine again," Hedz said.

Bonk mumbled something that sounded like, "rat fink."

"What?"

He resisted the urge to roll his eyes. "Sorry," he said automatically.

Hedz gave him a look. "If you don't put it down, anything can crawl down there. And if something comes up when I'm using it, you're not going to be very happy with the result."

Bonk, knowing the difference between an idle threat and a real one, nodded vigorously.

Hedz looked mollified. She looked up at the clouds again. "Looks like it's about ready."

Just then there was a major clap of thunder and the sky spigot opened up. Rain came flooding down.

Gop's man-fan group scattered, shouting, slipping and sliding down the hill whose surface instantly morphed to the viscosity of a Slip and Slide.

Hedz grabbed Eff, and Bonk followed them inside the cave.

Gop joined them, glaring resentfully at the rain now pouring down from the skies. "This was certainly inconvenient. Do you realize what it took to set up these interviews?"

"Sorry, Hon," Bonk said, his eyes on the storm. He looked at his mate, "Do you think we're going to get some lightning?"

As if in answer, lighting strobed the sky, lighting up the entire valley with a Kodak flash.

Hedz put Eff down, and squatted. "All we do now is wait until lightning hits a…"

Before she could complete the sentence, there was a gigantic crash, boom and cracking sound as lightning slammed into a mangrove tree near the river. A branch crashed to the ground and static electricity crackled around them, standing Hedz's freshly washed hair on end. Bonk's way more greased down hair proved more resistant to the pull of charged protons.

Bonk opened his eyes, which had closed entirely without his permission, and looked out at the tree. Sure enough, precious fire was flickering in the tree.

"Get it!" Hedz cried.

Bonk looked at the downpour. It was raining saber tooth cats and wolves. "Um, do I have to?"

"Yes," she snapped.

They both jumped as a cold blast of wind blew a gust of wet into the cave.

Bonk put on his most pitiful expression. "But it's cold and wet."

"You're the Fire God. The Carrier of Fire. Remember?"

She gestured at the lighting-shaped scar on his head. "And look. That scar looks just like a lightning bolt. You were meant to do this."

He felt the scar.

"And we will own fire which will give your family protection," Hedz added.

He nodded, rubbing at the goose pimples on his hairy arms. His teeth were chattering.

Hedz noticed. "And warmth. Fire will bring us warmth."

"Warmth?"

"Yep, our cave will be cozy and comfortable, rather than damp and chilly."

"Okay. Okay, you're right. I'll do it. I am the Fire God." He drew himself to full height, and bonked his noggin on the roof of the cave.

"Ow." He rubbed his head.

She hugged him. "That's my man. Take Frigg with you."

"Huh?"

"Your oldest son. He needs experience in matters like this."

She was right. As usual.

Bonk went into the cave. The boys were watching the fights on rock again. On the card tonight were a couple of pill bugs that were more interested in trying to get back under cover than in fighting to the death. The boys didn't care, just as content to watch the races instead of the fights. They were cheering for them to reach stain marks on the rocks, Bush helping their progress with prods from the snake stick. The snake wasn't quite as interested, seeing as there weren't any mice on the rock and pill bugs weren't very tasty.

"Frigg," Bonk said. "Hedz wants you to come with me to capture fire."

Frigg's eyes lit up, "Really?"

"Hey, how about me?" Bush cried.

"Nope, you weren't invited," Bonk said.

"Why not?" Bush whined.

Bonk shrugged. "Talk to the boss. Besides, it's raining. You won't like it. C'mon, Frigg."

When they got to the cave's entrance, Frigg balked at the sight of the downpour. "Um, maybe I don't want to…"

"Too bad," Bonk said. "If I gotta go, you gotta go." He looked into the storm. Then, gritting his teeth, he rushed into the cloudburst, brandishing his fire-capturing stick.

Frigg paused, and looked at Hedz for a last minute reprieve. But like a Texas governor at an execution, she shook her head and pointed.

He ran into the rain, screaming a mighty war cry."Aaagh!"

The rain hit him like a wave, choking off the war cry and drenching him in the first instant. Then, carried by water, the ground rushed out from under him and he smacked into the mud, momentum carrying him down the side of the hill. "Whoa!" he cried, sliding down the hill like a river otter. Halfway down he caught up to Bonk who had nearly speared himself somewhere sensitive on a boulder.

The mudslide carried them the rest of the way, depositing them gently onto the path. There they scrambled to their feet, digging long nailed toes into the slushy coating floating on what was normally a stable surface. Finally upright, Bonk looked around for the flaming tree. Ah, there it was.

Somehow he'd retained possession of his stick, so with Frigg following, they got off the path onto the grass lining the path. The grass's roots were holding the turf in place, so the footing was much better. Bonk looked up at the cave, and could just see his mate watching through the sheets of rain from the nice dry dimness of the cave's overhang.

He gave her a thumbs up.

"What's that?" Frigg asked.

Bonk looked at his thumb, wondering why he'd made the gesture.

"Um, I don't know."

Shrugging, he turned back to the tree.

The mangrove was large and white-barked, its exposed roots dipping to sip directly from the river. The lightning strike had blasted the trunk jaggedly in half, and a crackling fire was burning under a broken branch. Clouds of steam hissed from where fire wrestled water.

Bonk got as close as he dared, climbing into the heat. Rain beat on his shoulders and head. Frigg had retreated under a branch, huddled and shivering, trying to keep the worst of the rain off.

Remembering how he had first captured the fire, Bonk poked his stick into the heart of the fire. After a moment, he pulled it out.

Nothing, but the wood was drying. Heartened, he thrust the stick back into the flames. Meanwhile, water pelted his back and head, soaking his thick heavy hair. He felt miserable. But his mate wanted fire.

Suddenly, yellow flame flickered to life near the end of his stick. Tentatively, he pulled the stick out again. This time, a merry flame was dancing on the end.

Heart pounding, he let the flame grow, watching until it engulfed the end of his stick.

Fire!

He jumped down. "C'mon."

They ran towards the cave, where Hedz could just dimly be seen watching through the downpour. "We have fire! We have fire! We have fire!"

But the pounding rain warred with his fledging flame and after a brief struggle, the fire succumbed with a weak sizzle.

Frigg grabbed Bonk's arm. "The fire went out."

Bonk slid to a stop.

"Huh?"

"The fire is gone."

"Ahhhh!"

They ran back towards the tree.

"We don't have fire! We don't have fire! We don't have fire!"

When they got back to the tree, Bonk thrust the stick back into the flames. After a moment, flame popped into being.

They ran back towards the cave.

"We have fire!"

The flame petered out.

"We don't have fire!"

They headed back to the tree.

160

A moment later, flame jumped back onto the branch.

Back to the cave.

"We have fire!"

The fire quenched.

"We don't have fire!"

"We have fire!"

"We don't have fire!"

When they got back to the tree the final time, they paused, considering their options. The rain was the problem. If they could just keep the flame burning until the rain stopped.

Then Frigg remembered.

"Use the other charm."

Bonk frowned. "What other charm?"

"The one that stops rain! Remember? He gave us two charms."

"That's right," Bonk exclaimed. Seeing as he had no pockets, he had tied the charm into his hair. He untied it, and rubbed it to release the magic.

The rain stopped.

"Yay, we have fire! We have fire! We have fire!"

They whooped and hooted, and took off sloshing through the mud to the cave.

A few steps later something else started falling from the sky.

Hail.

Big, marble-sized chunks of ice.

"OwOwoOwOwOwOwOw!"

A few minutes later, two bruised, bleeding, muddy but happy cavemen entered the cave, triumphantly brandishing flame.

"Quick, get it in something that burns," Hedz said. She pointed at some rushes. "Gop, gather some of those reeds and put them on the floor over there."

Gop grabbed a handful of excess rushes gathered from when they were refreshing their sleeping pit, and dumped them on the floor.

"These burn fast, so we need some wood, too," Hedz instructed.

Next to the mouth of the cave was a big pile of wood used to barricade the cave from predators. Gop piled some on top of the rushes.

Hedz critically studied the result.

She nodded. "Okay, it's ready for the flame."

Bleeding and dripping, a grinning Bonk jammed the flaming end of the stick into the combustible pile. The flame eagerly flicked onto the rushes, running up the leaves with fiery delight. Within seconds, the rushes were blazing. With some crackling and popping, flame caught on the wood, and soon there was a merry blaze warming up the mouth of the cave.

"Whoa," Bush said, emerging from the interior of the cave.

"Where's the baby?" Hedz snapped. The boys were taking turns watching their sister as punishment for nearly losing her to the crocodile.

"Got her," Bush said. Eff was nestled in one hairy arm and he was carrying his walking snake stick in the other.

The cave family crowded around the fire, enjoying the dry warmth.

Then Hedz took a sniff. "What's that smell?"

Bonk and the boys looked at each other and shrugged.

Hedz leaned into her mate, sniffed, and a look of distaste spread over her face. "It's you. You stink."

Bonk sniffed under an armpit. "Wha..?"

"You smell like wet caveman," Hedz accused. She sniffed Frigg. "You do, too."

"I am a wet caveman," Bonk said. He grinned. "Besides, I'm drying pretty quickly, thanks to my fire."

"Maybe, but now you smell like moldy caveman."

Bonk frowned, "What's wrong with that?"

She held her nose. "The only thing worse smelling than a caveman is a wet, moldy caveman."

Bush grinned, loving the direction the conversation was taking.

Eff reached a chubby hand out for the snake at the end of the walking stick with the intent on sticking it her mouth.

The snake didn't look particular enthused at the prospect of getting gummed and it pooped nervously.

Outside, the rain stopped as quickly as it had arrived. Black clouds scurried through the sky, revealing a tapestry of blue sky.

Hedz grinned wickedly. Then she grabbed Bonk and Frigg and towed them outside.

"Wha…?" they cried.

Hedz dragged them into the steamy after-rain. Big fat drops splattered from the trees onto wet mud.

Bonk tried to resist but his mate was too strong. "What are you doing?!"

Frigg moaned, knowing something horrible was about to ensue.

"You two are getting a bath," Hedz said with a grim smile. "NOOOOOOOOOOOOOO!!!!!!!!!"

Chapter 36

The next morning was fresh and clean, the sun bright and cheery, quickly drying last night's mud to a cement-like consistency. Bonk walked along the river to the Guys Club Meeting Place at the Portsbar.

As he walked, he rejoiced in the beauty of the day, feeling he should be doing something special. Whistling, maybe. But, alas, whistling was not yet invented. So he pursed his lips and blew softly, enjoying the clean air. Of course, he'd never experienced pollution, with the exception of whenever the volcano got cranky and emitted smog rivaling that of future factories once lobbyists paid politicians to relax emission controls.

Bonk climbed onto the croc-barrier rocks and scrambled until he was on top. There was a small gathering of cavemen lounging on the rocks. It was the usual group, with the addition of Lob, the newcomer who had recently been consorting with Area Wug on matters relevant to the tribe.

Bonk waved a greeting to his friends. "Howdy, fellow troglodytes."

"Uh, man, what happened to you?" Droog said, holding his nose.

Bonk froze. "What?"

"You reek of clean. What's up?"

"Oh, that. Um. Well, Hedz sort of …" Unwilling to complete the sentence, he interrupted himself brightly. "Hey, I discovered fire again."

"Again?" Area Wug frowned from his place on higher rocks overlooking the other cavemen.

"Yep, I found it once before and lost it…"

"Yeah, he lost it on my Woodhenge," Dork interrupted, looking up from a barnacle he had been examining.

Bonk flushed, "Well, that's right. But it was a mistake."

"Though maybe a fortuitous mistake," Dork said. "We found out cooked meat tastes really good."

" Cooked?" Wug asked.

"Yes, cooked. When you put fire on meat, the meat turns brown and chewy, releasing a most wonderful smell."

"Interesting," Wug said. "We'll convene a committee to examine your claims." He turned to address everyone. "In the meantime, we have a serious situation. Berp?"

He turned. Where was his assistant?

Berp climbed out from behind some rocks. The cavemen looked up and gawked.

Berp had lashed sticks together into a throne-like chair that fitted onto his narrow shoulders. Sitting like royalty on the seat, looking around nearsightedly, was the platypus. God. Smelling the nearby sea, the little animal got excited and tried scrambling off the platform. Berp stuck out a hand, saving the platypus from a drop onto the rocks.

"All hail, God," Wug intoned.

The cavemen just stared, mouths open.

Lob appeared next to Wug, who barely jumped. He was getting used to Lob's method of arrival.

"Tell them to get on their knees and pray," Lob hissed.

Wug nodded. "On your knees. We must worship him."

The cavemen hesitated.

"On your knees, or God will punish you," Wug thundered.

Nobody wanted punishment, so the cavemen scrambled to their knees.

"Now what?" Bonk asked.

"Say, 'repeat after me'" Lob whispered into Wug's ear.

"Repeat after me," Wug cried.

"You are God. You are great," Lob hissed.

"You are God. You are great," Wug yelled at the cavemen.

"You are God. You are great," the cavemen chimed.

They weren't talking to the platypus. Instead, their eyes were on Area Wug who frowned. "Talk to the God, not me."

"Oh, sorry," they said. All eyes swung to the platypus, whose attention was on a dragonfly.

"Tell them to say, 'We worship you," Lob whispered into Wug's ear.

"Say, 'We worship you," Wug instructed.

"We worship you."

"We will sacrifice to you," Lob whispered hoarsely.

"We will sacrifice to you," Wug faithfully repeated.

The cavemen didn't know the word 'sacrifice,' but after a pause, they obediently said, "We will sacrifice to you."

"Amen," Lob said into Wug's ear.

"Amen," Wug said.

"Amen."

They all stood there.

"Amen' means you're done now. You can sit," Wug said.

"Oh, okay." The cavemen resumed their reclining positions on the rocks.

When they were all comfortable ... well, as comfortable as you can get on rocks, Droog asked, "What's this 'sacrifice' thing?"

Wug looked startled. "Um, well, it's when… um …"

Lob spoke up for the first time, "Sacrifice is when you kill something to prove your loyalty and obedience to a higher being."

The cavemen thought about this.

"Um, are you saying we should kill something, and then give it to God?" Droog asked.

166

"Yes," Lob said.

"So God wants me to kill a squirrel for it?" Deth asked.

"Yes," Lob responded.

"Does God want an antelope?" Tacks asked.

Lob hesitated, then said, "Yes."

Deth raised a finger. "But aren't the animals also God's creatures? Why would He want us to kill His other creations?"

Lob glared. "We are his Chosen. All animals are made for our purposes."

"If He made them in the first place, why does He want us to give them back to Him?" Tacks asked.

"He just does," Lob growled.

The cavemen looked doubtfully at the little platypus.

"What, uh, does God do with the animals we sacrifice?" Deth asked.

"It doesn't matter," Lob replied. "It is not for us to understand the motives of God."

The cavemen thought about that.

"Are each of us supposed to bring Him something or can we offer a joint sacrifice?" Tacks asked.

"Each of you must contribute," Lob answered, no pause this time.

Deth picked up a rock and tossed it into the water. Then, carefully not looking at Lob, he ventured, "So let's say on a good day, I bring a squirrel. Tacks brings an antelope, Bonk brings a … a … " Deth looked at Bonk. They all knew Bonk wasn't much of a hunter. "… a mouse," Deth continued, grinning.

Bonk shot him a glare.

Deth ignored the death ray and concluded, "So all of us are supposed to bring sacrifices and pile them in front of God. So we do this. What exactly happens to this big, huge pile of food?"

"We cut out the hearts, of course," Lob said, as if they were dummies.

"What happens to the rest of the food?" Deth asked.

"We throw it away," Lob answered.

That brought more silence. Cavemen didn't lightly discard food.

Droog looked at Wug and cocked a finger at Lob, "Where'd you get this guy?"

"Hey!" Wug said. "A little respect here."

They all grumbled a bit about that.

Finally, Wug interrupted the griping. "Look, God is God. You don't want to anger Him. Do you want Him to release thunder, earthquakes and devastation on us?"

"We already get that stuff," Tacks replied.

"Well, we don't want worse than that. How about flooding, hurricanes? There's a lot of nasty stuff out there. And now we have God here to protect us. So we're going to take care of Him. Got it?"

He glared at them.

"Yeah, yeah," they finally grumbled.

Wug looked mollified. "Okay, now that that's resolved, we have another serious matter to discuss. As we discussed last meeting, the Meefs are arming themselves."

"So?" Droog retorted.

Wug frowned. "We need to be prepared for invasion."

There was a collective gasp from the cavemen.

"Who are the Meefs?" Deth asked.

"The squirrel cavemen," Berp responded. The platypus above him seemed to nod.

"Ohhhh…" the cavemen chorused.

Tacks scratched somewhere indelicate. "How do we get ready?"

"Like I said last meeting, we raise an army," Wug declared.

"How high?" Droog asked.

Wug frowned. "Huh?"

"How high do we raise them?" Droog asked.

"Like, do we put them on the trees?" Deth asked.

"I hate climbing trees," Tacks said.

"Though we're pretty good at it," Droog pointed out.

"No, no, no!" Wug shouted. "We don't put them in trees."

"Then do we raise them the way we raised our children?" Bonk asked.

"I was raising some corn," Deth said.

The other cavemen looked at him.

Tacks snickered. "Hah, are you a gatherer now?"

Deth shook his head. "No way. I'm a hunter. I didn't want to farm. My mate made me."

Area Wug leaned over to Berp, "Would you get these idiots under control?"

Berp stood up and nearly lost his balance, causing the platypus to dig claws in the throne. "Hey, stupids. Pay attention to the boss."

"Boss? Who made him boss?" Droog asked. "It's one thing to vote the ladies out, but who voted him boss?"

"Who said anything about voting at all?" Berp snapped back.

"I think we vote for a leader," Droog said.

"Fine with me," Wug growled.

Then Lob whispered into his ear.

Wug nodded. "Okay, here's how it's going to work. The day disk is on its way down. We will accept discourse by anyone who wants his say about whether I continue as leader or if we vote in a new leader. Sound fair?"

The cavemen thought about it and couldn't see any flaws.

Wug nodded and continued. "And if the day disk goes down without a vote or there being a decision to vote, I remain leader. Okay?"

The nods were more tentative this time.

"Who wants to talk first?" Wug said.

Berp's and Droog's hands shot up.

Wug ignored Droog and pointed to Berp.

"Okay, you're first up."

Berp shrugged out of the platypus-carrying platform, and put God down carefully on a pile of dry kelp. The platypus began nibbling on the seaweed.

"I, Berp, son of Herb and Bev, grandson of Bek and Orei, great-grandson of Ruch and Chen, great-great-grandson of Rea and Dub…"

An hour later, Berp had moved on to his eating habits, "… I like to eat antelope, weasel, armadillo, grass rat …

An hour later, the cavemen were fighting sleep as Berp discussed the places he liked to hunt.

An hour later, Berp was still going on.

Wug yawned deeply and whispered to Lob, "What do you call this again?"

Lob whispered back, "It's called a fillseatbuster. That means we bust up their votes by talking and keeping them in their seats. All we have to do is just keep talking until the time runs out."

He looked up at the day disk. It was rapidly sliding down the sky. "Which should be any time soon."

Meanwhile, Berp was regaling the cavemen with stories of his exploits as a kid. "…and then I hit my sister with the club and her eyes crossed … ha, ha, … and, well, she never was the same after that … and …"

Gloom overtook the Portsbar as the day disk slipped over the horizon.

When it had totally disappeared, Wug hopped up where he had been snoozing and grinned broadly. "Ah, a successful fillseatbuster. Berp, you can stop now."

But Berp was in full monologue, "… then there was the time when I was a baby and I wanted a rattle, so I crawled out into the desert and took one from a snake …"

Wug shrugged his immense shoulders, and looked for Lob.

The little caveman was nowhere in sight. God was sleeping off His dinner of hermit crabs. The cavemen were mostly snoring. Wug listened to them for a second. They were actually snoring in harmony. He made a mental note to suggest this new kind of singing in the next meeting.

Then he remembered he never remembered mental notes. That's why he had an assistant. He turned to tell Berp to remember snore-singing, but the caveman was still monologuing.

"… and my parents said they had never seen such a cute baby, and I was embarrassed, but I knew they were right, so …"

Wug shook his head sadly. Why did he have to do everything, himself?

In his huge voice, he thundered, "Wake up, everyone!"

The cavemen jerked, and looked around in confusion.

Wug waited until they had rubbed the sleep out of their eyes. "All right. This council meeting is over. I announce that since there was no decision to vote, I remain boss."

"Wha…" Droog asked, rubbing his eyes tiredly.

"Oh, no, we missed our chance," Bonk cried. He stretched, popping his back. He had been sleeping with his shoulder wedged into a rocky crevasse.

"Be back here first thing in the morning," Wug shouted. He dropped onto the sand and headed for his cave.

Sleepy and grumbling, the other cavemen followed, except heading for their own caves instead.

Berp kept talking.

A bit before dawn, it dawned on him he had lost his audience, so he quietly gathered up the peacefully sleeping God, and went to put the platypus on its ledge.

Chapter 37

Later that night, Hedz was awakened by grunting, sniffing and snorting. Groggily, she rolled away from her mate. "Not now, Bonk. I'm tired."

"Huh?" Bonk asked. While sleeping, he had somehow gotten wedged between the two boys and his face was snuggled up against Frigg's filthy feet.

Hedz realized the noise was coming from the cave entrance. Something was sniffing around the drying fire, trying to muster the nerve to shove its way into the cave. Whatever it was, it didn't mind the stench of a family of mostly unwashed cavemen, which either meant it was olfactory-challenged or just hungry enough not to care.

One of the branches in the fire was tugged sharply, releasing a spray of sparks. The animal growled and backed away.

The commotion woke the boys.

"Wha…?" Frigg said, squinting into the dark..

Hedz crawled out of the sleeping pit, and hissed, "Get some more wood on the fire."

Something was stalking back and forth on the other side of the fire, probing for weaknesses. It was ominously silent, but they could sense its huge bulk.

"Wolverine," Bonk said.

That was bad. A wolverine was the biggest member of the weasel family. A fearsome hunter, its jaws were powerful enough to crunch through bone. A ravenous wolverine could take down a moose and would eat everything, including antlers, fur and teeth.

Bonk grabbed a spear and slid up behind the branches and fire barrier.

Frigg dragged a handful of branches from a pile in the cave and shoved it into the flames. The wolverine snarled and wedged its flat head past some branches where the fire was weakest.

Bush shoved his walking stick at the wolverine.

"What are you doing?" Bonk asked.

"I think my snake's poisonous. I'm trying to get him to bite," Bush said.

When the snake saw the wolverine, its eyes went wide and it pooped.

Bush saw the brown pebbles coming out of the snake's butt and he shook the stick, dropping little snake pellets over the wolverine. "Pooh on you."

Finally, the fire caught on the new brush and flared to life.

The wolverine barked in frustration and backed away, eyes reflecting the light.

"Yah!" Bonk yelped, brandishing his spear.

"Jorj you," Frigg shouted.

"Pooh on you," Bush yelled, rattling the snake stick.

"Goo Goo," Eff cried, reaching for a pretty burning ember.

"Gop," Hedz shrieked. "Get the baby!'

Gop swooped under the boys and snatched the baby.

The fire flared higher and with a last snarl, the predator reluctantly turned tail, disappearing into the darkness.

"We have to keep this fire built up at nights," Hedz said into the silence left behind by the overgrown weasel.

"I'll do it," Lump said from her usual spot near the sleeping pit.

They looked at the old lady with surprise. Lump rarely moved, usually just sitting placidly in the darkness of the cave like, well, a lump.

"Are you sure, Old Mother?" Hedz asked.

"Sure," Lump said. "These lazy old bones don't let me do much, but sitting beside a warm fire all night won't hurt me at all. You all can tend it during the day and I'll catch up my sleep then."

Chapter 38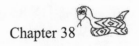

"I have a sad announcement," Area Wug said into the sea breeze at the Portsbar after most of the tribe's cavemen had arrived. Seeing as the women had been deprived of the right to vote, there was no need to convene the entire tribe to discuss important events. And since Wug had been confirmed by fillseatbuster as sole leader, he almost had decided to simply meet with himself to determine tribe policy. But it would take as much effort to implement rules afterward as it would be to announce them here. Plus he enjoyed issuing public proclamations, which was a bit difficult if there was no one present to hear.

The cavemen paused their morning scratch-fest and looked up curiously.

Wug put on a doleful expression.

"God died last night."

A collective gasp.

"He sacrificed Himself to save us from a horrible predator," Wug continued.

Gasp again.

Wug gestured and Berp dragged out a large furry body. A massive wolverine, its coat thick and shaggy. Its flat muzzle was gaping open, something jammed deep into its throat.

The platypus.

Another collective gasp.

Wug looked "This killer showed up last night to devour me, and God threw Himself into the wolverine's mouth and did Godly battle."

176

The truth was the wolverine had seen the platypus on the ledge and thinking it a handy snack, simply snapped it up. But the platypus's wide duck beak had gotten lodged in the wolverine's esophagus and the more the wolverine struggled, the deeper the platypus was wedged. And because the platypus was frantically stabbing the wolverine the whole time with the poisonous barb on his foot, the wolverine had been too confused and distracted to dislodge the small mammal. Or whatever a platypus is.

Wug bowed his head.

"Everyone bow," Berp shouted.

Casting dubious glances at each other, the cavemen bowed.

Wug lifted his head back up and gazed at the sky with piety, "God is great. God is good. Long live God."

"Um, I thought God is dead," Droog pointed out.

Wug's head snapped down. "You know what I mean."

"Think he'll come back to life?" Droog asked.

"Don't be ridiculous," Wug snapped.

"Hey, can I have the wolverine fur?" Droog asked.

Wug frowned, "What? No, it's mine."

"Okay, can I have God's fur then?" Droog asked.

"Of course not," Wug shouted. "It's sacred."

"Well, I thought He was the God of all of us, so how do you know which one of us should get the sacred fur?" Droog asked reasonably.

"Because," Wug said, thinking furiously.

Lob showed up from somewhere and whispered in his ear.

Wug nodded. "Because His Holy Ghost spoke to me. I was His chosen one. That's why He saved me."

No one could argue because the platypus had, in fact, died outside of Wug's cave.

"Anyway," Wug said, quickly shoving the topic aside. "As we discussed before the, um, sky disk departed, um …"

"Yesterday," Dork put in.

Wug frowned, "What?"

Dork scratched a particularly itchy part of his epidermis. "I invented the word. It means the day before."

"What's day?" Bonk asked curiously. This was falling in line with his ideas to invent measurements of time.

"Day is when the day disk is overhead, bringing us warmth," Dork responded.

Bonk nodded, liking this. "And what about when it's fallen from the sky?"

"That's called 'night,'" the caveman inventor replied.

"Perfect," Bonk said. "So we have day and night. So what's this 'yesterday' thing?"

"Yesterday is the day that already happened," Dork said.

"So any time before now is yesterday?" Deth asked.

Dork started to speak, paused, then said, "Well, no, not exactly. Yesterday is the day before, but not the day before the day before. Or the days before that."

Deth's eyebrows beetled. "Huh?"

"So what are those days called?" Bonk asked.

"I don't know yet. I haven't gotten that far yet," Dork admitted.

"Why not?" Deth asked. "What do we pay you for anyway?"

"You don't pay me at all," Dork retorted. "Though, now that I'm thinking about it, maybe you should."

"Well, it's certainly an improvement over what we have right now," Wug interrupted, not liking the sound of currency going somewhere other than in his direction. "Nice job, Dork."

Dork grinned, pleased.

Bonk wasn't quite ready to let go of what was one of his favorite thinking pastimes. "Okay, so yesterday is the day before. Is there a yesternight?"

Dork's pleased grin evaporated. "Uh, well, no."

"What's a yester anyway?" Deth asked.

"It's, er, an amalgamation of yes and, um …" Dork stuttered.

Area Wug stood, his vast bulk getting their attention. "We're getting off subject," he proclaimed. "Quiet down."

The cavemen settled down.

When he had everyone's attention again, he continued. "Now, if you remember, it was brought to my attention that our neighbors the Meefs have taken up arms and are preparing to attack us.

"The Meefs?" Bonk asked. "But they're so little."

"I could crush them," Deth cried, flexing long arms that nearly went down to the ground.

"Perhaps," Wug said. "But my information …"

They all looked at Lob. Wug never went very far from his cave. They knew Lob was the source of his information.

Wug continued, "My information is that the Meefs are developing WMD!"

The cavemen gasped.

Bonk looked around at the other cavemen. They looked clueless. So he raised a finger, "What's 'WMD?"

The other cavemen looked relieved someone had asked what they were all thinking.

Wug glowered at Bonk. "Weapons of mass destruction."

The cavemen gasped again.

Then there was silence.

After a moment, Bonk looked around again, then asked sheepishly,

"Um, what are weapons of mass destruction?"

Wug opened his mouth to speak, realized the necessary information was not in his brain, turned to Lob and whispered, "what are…"

179

"I heard the question," Lob snapped. When he saw the startled look on the chieftain's face, his tone softened. "They have spears," he said.

"Oooo, the most advanced weaponry ever," Deth said.

"Yeah, way more versatile than clubs," Tacks said.

Deth pursed his lips, "I dunno, clubs still have their strong points."

"Clubs don't have any points," Bonk said.

"You know what I mean. Clubs work better on animals like baby seals."

"Yeah, someday we'll have a better more humane way to kill baby seals," Tacks said.

Deth smacked a fist into his palm, "Maybe, but for now clubbing works just fine."

"We were talking about spears," Lob interrupted.

"We have spears," Bonk said.

Lob spared him a disdainful look, "No, you have pointed sticks. They have spears."

"I don't get it," Bonk aid.

Area Wug gestured, and a solitary caveman stood up and moved to join the chief.

"Steve?" Droog whispered to Bonk.

Bonk just shrugged.

"I'm sure you're all wondering what Steve's doing up here," Wug said.

The cavemen nodded. Steve was the most worthless of cavemen. What would he have to do with a discussion about war?

Wug waved at another cavemen, "Dork, would you please explain?"

Dork stood, "Well, Steve here is the closest thing we have to a modern human."

Silence.

Then the entire rock of cavemen erupted in laughter.

Deth wiped away tears, "We're the modern humans. I don't know what Steve is, but he ain't modern."

More laughter.

Dork waited until the laughter died, and continued unfazed. "Maybe we are modern now, but Steve will be modern later,"

"What are you talking about?" Tacks asked. "He's weak. He can't even hunt."

"None of us can hunt anymore," Deth said with venom.

They all nodded knowingly. Ever since the women had insisted on bathing their men, it was getting harder to sneak up on animals now that their natural smell wasn't masked by stench.

"I miss my lice," Tacks murmured.

They all nodded at that, too. Once something you lived with your whole life was taken away, you missed it, good or bad. Plus lice tasted good. Sometimes on a long fruitless hunt, they were a food source of last resort.

"Yeah," Tork added, "Anyway, Steve's not modern, he's defective. Look, his eyebrow doesn't even grow all the way across his face."

"Freak," Deth said.

"And he has that weird lack of hair on the top of his head," Tork pointed.

Deth nodded, 'And a flat face and those strange colored eyes,"

"He's like the cavemen of cavemen. A throwback, not a throw-forward," Tork concluded.

Steve simply watched the general condemnation of his habits, looks and heredity with the placid look of future accountants who knew they'd get revenge when it came time to bill for their services.

Dork, on the other hand, was getting angrier with every comment. "I'm getting angrier with every comment," he growled.

He looped a long arm around Steve's pasty rounded shoulders, "Steve has improved the spear."

"Improved how?" Bonk asked.

"With this," Dork said, shaking the spear that until that moment, no one had noticed him carrying.

A beauty.

"Ooo-ahhhh," the cavemen chorused.

Steve gently took the spear from Dork. "I used only the best hardwood, polished with fish oils. The spearhead is composed of chipped stone, ground to sharp edges and a point." He tapped the end. "Notice the barbs, which keep the spear from being easily displaced once it pierces the hide."

"How'd you get it to stick in the wood?" Bonk asked.

"Well, I don't want to tell you everything, but in a nutshell I make a groove in the wood, slide the end of the spearhead inside, and lash it with rawhide," Steve explained.

"Why don't you want to tell us everything?" Bonk asked.

"To be honest, I've decided to make a business of creating spears. And if I divulge the formula for how I cure the rawhide or my knot techniques, you would just make your own. I've copyrighted the technique," Steve added.

"What's that?" Tacks asked.

"Copyright means I'm the only one who can do it," Steve said.

"Or what?" Deth asked.

"Or the government will be all over you," Steve said with a glower.

Government.

Scary.

"Anyway," Steve continued. "My new company is going to create all of the spears for the army. No one else can do it."

182

Bonk frowned, "What's a company?"

"A company is a legal entity set up with corporate laws with the officers protected from personal liability. We hired Lob here to act as our intermediary with Chief Wug."

Lob nodded gravely and slipped a dead squirrel behind his back to Wug, who secreted it into the butt crack of the furs he had taken to wearing around his midsection.

"Which brings us to our army," Wug said. "We have instituted a draft."

Bonk scratched his nose. "A draft? Isn't that the wind that comes though the tunnel opening?"

"Well, no, I mean yes," Wug said.

"Those are homonyms," Dork said.

"Hommy-what?" Droog asked.

Dork drew himself up professorially, "A homonym is a word that has more than one meaning."

"Like to, too and two?" Bonk asked.

"Well, not quite. Those are homophones," Dork responded. "Homophones are words that are pronounced the same but have different meanings."

"Wait," Bonk said. "Okay, a draft is a wind, but you can also have a draft of beer which some genius will create some day. Plus there's that draft thing you're talking about now. So they are words pronounced the same with different meanings."

"The difference is homophones are spelled differently," Dork said.

"Oh," the cavemen chorused.

They didn't really understand, but they wanted to move on to the subject of fighting and armies and weapons. They were, after all, guys.

Wug took the hint, "Like I said, we're instituting a draft. This means that we … and by we I mean me .. will choose people to be in the army."

Silence as the cavemen digested this.

Wug continued, "We will have a standing army to defend our territory and our women."

Deth raised a hand, "We have to stand?"

"Is this related to the raising thing?" Tacks asked.

Wug shook his head impatiently, "No, you won't stand. That's a figure of speech."

Tacks interrupted, "Is this another one of those homo things?"

"No!" Wug shouted.

"Actually, he might be right," Dork said. "A standing army is a prepared army, not one that's always on its feet."

"I dunno, I'm not always on my feet," Deth said. "Sometimes I walk on all fours."

They looked at him.

Deth colored.

Then Wug continued, "Anyway, I'm going to choose our army right now. Anyone assigned to the army will be excused from hunting and gathering."

There was a babbling as everyone tried to talk at once.

"But what will we eat?" Tacks asked.

"It's not fair," Droog shouted.

"Shhhh," Wug commanded. "We have it all thought out. Some of you will be in the army. Others will be responsible for hunting and gathering. Each person not assigned to the army will be responsible for giving half of their hunt to the general fund, which will be split up among those in our army."

"It's called a tax," Lob put in.

"Wait a minute," Lunk interrupted. "I'm the most prolific hunter here. If I give up half of my hunt, I will be contributing way more than Bonk."

"Hey!" Bonk protested.

The other cavemen nodded. They knew Bonk wasn't a very good hunter.

184

"And how about me?" Tork asked. "I hunt big dangerous game. There's way more risk and my game provides way more meat."

Wug just shook his head, "Everyone will be taxed equally based on their skills."

"No way," Lunk shouted. "I'll bring in two armfuls of squirrels and rabbits, and Bonk gets off with, what three mice?"

"Hey!" Bonk said.

"And I'll bring in a woolly rhino all by myself, but it counts the same as a handful of squirrels?" Tork cried.

"Hey!" Lunk said.

"Yes, that's it exactly," Wug shouted. "No one said taxes have to be fair. They're not. So stop bellyaching about it!"

Bonk pointed at Steve, who was probably the only hunter less skilled than him. "How about Steve?"

"Steve's new company Caveaburton will be the single supplier of arms to our army. He will be paid from the General Fund created by taxes," Berp said.

Bonk's eyebrows shot into his hairline. "And how much does he get paid?"

"Whatever I decide he gets," Wug said, pocketing another squirrel slipped to him by Lob.

Lunk stood up, "There shouldn't be taxation without representation!"

Wug's big head swiveled towards the caveman. "You are represented."

"By who?" Lunk shot back.

"You mean, 'whom," Bonk interrupted.

"By me," Wug said to Lunk, his gaze taking in all the cavemen. "I'm representing you."

Lunk's big eyebrows beetled. "But aren't you the one taxing us?"

"Yes," Wug said. "And I'm representing you, too, so you know your best interests are protected."

"What else are you going to do with the taxes?" Bonk asked slowly.

"What?" Wug said.

"You're going to use it to pay for Defense. What about other social programs?"

Wug's eyebrows shot up. "What social programs?"

"How about feeding our poor? Our injured? Remember when Marg broke his leg and couldn't hunt?"

"So?"

"So as a community we should take care of him," Bonk said.

"That's welfare!" Lob shouted.

Bonk spun around and faced down the little caveman. "Exactly. That's what welfare means. Taxes should be used for the welfare of the individuals in our community. For schools, hospitals…"

"What's a hospital?" Deth asked.

"The witchdoctor's cave," Dork answered.

"Oh."

Bonk had a head of steam going. "As a group, we should all contribute to the community, so each of us is fed, strong, educated. Those who can't take care of themselves, like the elderly, need our help."

"I thought we just left old people on top of the mountain during the winter to die," Tacks said.

"We do, but that's not right," Bonk said passionately, thinking of the old woman Lump in his cave. "We should treasure them for their experience and knowledge, and give them the social security they deserve."

"Can I tax the social security?" Wug asked.

"Of course not!" Bonk retorted.

Lob leaned over and whispered into Area Wug's ear, the movement covering him covertly slipping a rabbit to the Chief.

Wug nodded and stood up, "Okay, as leader I've thought about it. I have listened to both sides, which means this will be a fair ruling. We shall continue to tax to fund our number one priority, defense."

"And social programs?" Bonk asked.

"Anyone else got anything to say?" Wug said, ignoring the question.

Suddenly, there was a scrabbling sound on the rocks on the shore. Everyone looked up just in time to see a peacock flit across the rocks, closely pursued by a fox. In seconds, the prey and its pursuer were out of sight.

Wug's attention swung back to Bonk. "And I wouldn't worry about it too much if I were you. You're the first draftee in our brand new army."

Bonk's eyes popped wide. "What?"

Wug pointed to Droog, "And you're in too."

Droog pointed to himself. "Me?" he squeaked.

"Yes," Wug said. "After all, you're the most expendable cavemen we have."

"What?!" Bonk and Droog cried in unison.

Dork shook his head, "I don't know about this. I'm not sure we should trust Bonk with advanced weaponry."

"What?!" Bonk cried.

Lob stood, "No, don't worry about it. The NSA will give anyone, even an idiot like Bonk, the right to bear arms. In fact, the NSA will specialize in idiots."

"What?" Bonk cried again.

"What's the NSA?" Droog asked.

"The National Spear Association," Lob said. "It's a little organization I started." He slipped another rabbit behind his back to the Chief, who quickly stowed it away.

"Yes," Wug thundered. "The Second Amendment gives every caveman the right to bear arms, independent to service in the army."

"What's the Second Amendment?" Droog asked.

"It's an amendment we will be creating once we create a law of the land," Wug said impatiently.

"Oh," Droog said.

They thought that over, but no one wanted to challenge it for fear of looking like an idiot.

Finally, Bonk stood up, "I'm not sure how I feel about all this. And what will Hedz say about this?"

"Look," Berp responded. He'd been quiet through most of the discussion. "You suck as a hunter. You probably won't make a very good soldier either, but consider this. You will be well paid in the currency of the day and serving Caveman-kind at the same time."

"Currency of the day?"

"Food, taken in taxes from our more prolific hunters," Berp gestured to Lunk and Tork, confusing them because they couldn't figure out whether to bask in the compliment or protest the inequitable taxation. In the end, they simply adapted the normal dumb look any guy takes on when he wants to appear inscrutable.

Chapter 39

"God died," Bonk announced, when he got back to the cave.

"That didn't take long," Hedz replied, busy tending the fire. She blew softly on the flame until it caught onto a branch. This caught Baby Eff's attention where she was sitting at Hedz's feet. The baby tried crawling towards the fire, but was stopped by a gentle nudge from her mother's foot. She settled back onto her butt, and popped a small rock into her mouth in a futile attempt to suck moisture from it.

"We're also creating an army," Bonk added as an aside.

At this, Hedz gave her mate a look. "Is that why you have a turtle shell on your head?"

Bonk reddened.

Hedz turned back to the fire, "Besides, it can't be much of an army if they let you be in it."

Bonk glowered. "Why does everyone keep saying that?!"

Hedz ignored this. "So why are you creating an army?"

"The Meefs," Bonk said sullenly.

This surprised her. "What about them?"

"They've taken up arms to invade us. So we have to prepare our defenses."

Hedz frowned. She remembered meeting Cheef and Deef, the leaders of the Meefs. They hadn't seemed at all warlike.

"Wug's going to have us attack first, something he called a pre-emptive strike."

"But what if they aren't really preparing for war?" Hedz asked.

189

Bonk shook his head, "Oh, Wug's pretty sure that when we invade them we'll find WMD there."

Hedz looked confused. "WMD?"

"Yes," Bonk said, delighted to know something his mate didn't know. "Weapons of Mass Destruction."

"What's a weapon of mass destruction?"

"Oh, you know, stuff. Like big boulders, spears. Lob said they have some kind of rocks tied together. And when you throw it at something, it wraps around their legs and trips them."

"Hmm," Hedz said thoughtfully.

Then someone thumped a club politely on the ground. Bonk and Hedz whirled, but relaxed when they saw it was their neighbor Gurt. He had a sheepish look on his face and was holding a shell. He also smelled freshly washed and cleaned. And he clearly wasn't happy about it.

"Um, Yerba sent me over to borrow a cup of fire," his eyes sliding over to admire the flame Hedz was tending.

Hedz smiled, "Sure, but you can't carry it in a cup."

"No? But Yerba said …"

"Nope, you need this." Hedz picked up the end of a branch whose other end was buried in flame. Holding it carefully, she handed the non-flaming end to the caveman, who flinched at the proximity of the flame. After a moment, when he realized it wasn't going to hurt him, he relaxed. He gazed into merry flame with fascination and held a hand near the fire.

A look of delight spread over his face. "It's warm."

"Yes," Hedz said. "And you must treat it like a baby and feed it often or it will die."

"Feed it? You mean like meat?" Gurt asked.

"You feed it wood, or grasses. The dryer the better, or you get a lot of smoke."

Gurt cast a doubtful eye on the flame, "We don't have to burp it, do we?"

190

Hedz laughed, "No, of course not. Just take care of it. And you can, in fact, feed it meat. Just put meat on a stick, immerse it in the fire and when you take it out, the meat is tasty, chewy and smells delicious."

"Wow," Gurt breathed. "Thanks."

He turned and walked away.

A few steps later, "OW!"

"But don't touch it," Hedz called out.

"Oh, okay," Gurt said. Then he jammed his burned finger in his mouth and headed for his cave, wondering why he all of a sudden felt an overwhelming desire for a marshmallow.

As he walked away, he wondered what a marshmallow was.

Perhaps he could find one in the swamp.

Chapter 40

Frigg and Bush were walking along an animal trail running along the ridge of the valley leading to the Meef village. When they had heard of the impending war, they, like any boys, were consumed with curiosity, so they decided they had to check out their neighbors.

As their feet slapped softly on the dirt, Frigg's eyes slid over to his brother who was intently trying to poke a thin stick into his snake's mouth.

"What are you doing?"

Bush flicked a glance at him, then back at the snake. The snake didn't look particularly enthused about getting poked. "I'm trying to figure out if he's poisonous."

"So you're testing this by seeing if he can kill a twig?" Frigg scoffed.

Bush kept gently probing. "Of course not, I'm trying to see if there's any venom. They have poison sacs at the base of their fangs."

Frigg was impressed, but wasn't about to admit it. "Where'd you learn that?"

"National Geographic."

"Huh?"

"It's a magazine that won't be invented for quite awhile. I just sort of borrowed the knowledge a bit before it existed."

"Huh?"

Bush tossed the twig onto the ground. "He's not poisonous. No wonder he didn't scare the wolverine."

192

"Nothing scares wolverines anyway," Frigg said. "Those suckers would take on a cave bear."

Rather than replying, Bush snagged a cricket that had wandered too close to the path and stuck it in the snake's face. The snake, recognizing food, opened its mouth to receive the gift. Bush crammed the cricket in, and the snake sucked it down. Bush watched until the wriggling legs disappeared."Hope he doesn't get dizzy on the end of the stick."

Frigg shot a glance at the snake. "I think if he were going to get sick, he would have already."

Bush blew out air, "Actually, I kind of wish he would. If he's not going to be poisonous, it'd be nice if he puked on people I don't like."

Frigg snickered, "I don't know. That 'poop on you' thing with the wolverine was pretty good."

"Yeah," Bush chortled. "If you can't kill 'em, poop on 'em." He looked at his snake who was keeping a steadfast eye on the path. "You're going to work out just fine, little guy."

"Shhh," Frigg suddenly hissed, dropping into a crouch.

Bush dived to the dirt.

In the caveman days, you didn't need to be warned twice to be careful. Well, some people did, but they usually got eaten fairly quickly. The survivors did their best to learn by this example.

"What's up?" Bush whispered, shuffling up next to his brother.

Frigg pointed at a small copse of trees nestled at the end of the valley below. "I think that's where the Meefs come from. Come on, let's get behind those rocks over there."

Below them, the valley led directly to the Meef village. Voracious mastodons used the path alongside the river to travel from one bit of green to another in their constant search for food. With nearby water, the place was perfect for the pachyderms. The woods and trail were strewn with broken branches and shredded trees tipped over by hungry elephants.

In and around the trees, small forms darted back and forth, plucking nuts and berries. Occasionally, a game of tag would ensue, with nimble forms chasing each other through the shadows.

Frigg frowned. "I don't see any weapons of mass destruction here."

"Maybe they're hiding them," Bush said doubtfully.

They watched for awhile longer. When nothing else developed, they backed away silently and made their way home.

Chapter 41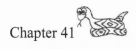

"So waddaya think?" Bonk asked proudly. He may not have been happy about the tax issue, but a snappy uniform cures a lot of doubt. He was standing, chest puffed out, clutching a new state-of-the-art spear, handcrafted by Steve from the defensive agency Caveaburton. The cost was several squirrels, but according to Wug, higher prices were the norm in defense spending. On Bonk's head was a shiny tortoise shell, and he was wearing an antelope hide cape with charcoal markings on the shoulders. The cape was drawn tight at the waist.

He knew he cut a dashing figure.

Somehow Hedz kept a straight face.

Bonk was standing at attention with arms still hanging down around his knees, wearing the same triumphant look Eff got whenever she got away with scarfing a bug. Said baby was trying to wrap her mouth around the butt of Bonk's state-of-the-art spear.

"What's that on your chest?" Hedz pointed at a wide piece of bark tied on with rawhide.

He grinned proudly. "Dork invented it. He called it armor."

Hedz dug her fingernails into her palms to keep from smiling. When the feeling passed, she stepped closer and reached towards the markings on his shoulders. "Let me just clean up those blotches on your outfit."

195

"No, you can't," Bonk cried, stepping backwards. He gestured to the chevrons with pride. "These are the insignia of my rank."

Hedz frowned. "You don't smell rank anymore. We took care of that with the bath."

Bonk's lips twisted. "Not that kind of rank. Rank, like hierarchy, like who's in charge. I'm a private." He straightened as much as he could, seeing as how cavemen backs weren't particularly suitable for standing up straight.

When she didn't respond, he added, "That's private first class."

Hedz smiled. "Oh, yeah, you're definitely first class." She looked down the hill. Other cavemen similarly clad as Bonk were streaming towards a small clearing near the path, where other cavemen were milling around. "Well, looks like your friends are ready to play soldier. Go ahead and join them."

Bonk gave her a look. "We're not playing."

"Okay," Hedz said.

"This is important stuff. We need to protect you womenfolk."

"Of course," she said with a straight face.

Bonk had expected a bit of a fight, and her quiescence knocked him a bit off stride.

When she said nothing else, he cleared his throat. "Okay, got to go."

She nodded.

"Dangerous stuff," he added.

"I know," she agreed.

With a soft pop, Bonk carefully pulled the butt end of the spear out of his daughter's toothless maw. He shook off the drool, and then whirled and started marching down the hill. After a few militarily precise steps, he broke rank with himself and ran the rest of the way.

As Hedz watched her man go to war, she wondered what it was about the male species that required such constant display of aggression mixed with idiocy mixed with childishness.

There was a rumbling from the sky, and she looked up to see how far away the storms were. To her surprise, the sky was clear. There was a second rumbling and this time there were vibrations in the ground. Curious, she looked over at the volcano. The smoke seemed thicker than normal. Hmm, weird. She shrugged and turned to go back into the cave.

Just then, two somethings slid down the hill like major league baseball players stealing third.

"You won't believe what we saw," Frigg's voice said from a cloud of dust.

"We checked out the Meefs," Bush added. He pulled himself up with the help of his walking stick.

The snake on the end coughed from all of the dirt and debris. Hedz looked more carefully. Snakes don't cough. The snake looked unblinkingly back at her. She decided she must have been hearing things.

She looked at dusty son number two. "What do you mean you checked out the Meefs?"

"We spied on their village. They aren't preparing to fight anybody."

"Yeah," Frigg said. "They were just playing in the trees. There weren't any weapons."

Hedz looked down the hill at the soldiers. Berp was frantically trying to corral the erstwhile soldiers into a line with the same lack of success had they been pill-bugs.

She decided she would investigate the Meefs herself.

Chapter 42

Area Wug climbed a downed log in front of the river. He looked nervously into the swirling water for crocs, but the big female was gone. After her babies had left the nest, she had vacated soon after the women had started bathing their cavemen in the river, raising the toxicity levels past crocodile tolerance limits. There was a lingering oily residue on the river that gave hint of future BP Amoco and Exxon spills.

At the top of the log, Wug steadied himself and turned to face the caveman army, which was milling around the clearing jabbering amongst themselves. He took a deep breath to yell for their attention … but then something else stole their attention with an effectiveness Wug could not even begin to compete with.

Young cave women.

Gop, Sheez and several other of the young nubile cave girls were swaying down the path.

Every single guy stopped what he was doing.

Jaws dropped.

Several moments passed as their alleged male brains attempted to regain motor control of their mouths which had been stunned into inertness when all nerve impulses had been abruptly reassigned to their optic nerves.

Finally, the appropriate synapses fired.

"Whoa," they breathed in unison like an all-male choir.

The girls marched single-file, hips swinging, young cleavages trying to burst out of their newfound confinement. When they reached the group of men, they spread out as if on

198

an imaginary cakewalk and stopped, faces flushed, bosoms heaving.

Sheez let them ogle for a minute, and smiled seductively, "Hi, boys."

Puddles of drool were making mud at the cavemen's feet.

"Look," Sheez said. "We heard about this hunting taxing thing."

She paused, but no one said anything.

"And the girls and me ..." she started.

"You mean, 'and I,'" another girl whispered.

A bright smile flashed on Sheez's face, "That's right. Grammar is important to ladies. Yes, the girls and I have been thinking how cruel hunting is."

Deth found his voice, "Bu.., but we have to hunt."

Sheez stunned him into a mild form of statue-itis with a radiant smile. "No, we don't. There's another way to eat."

Gop nodded, "Gathering. There are so many nuts, roots and berries. We don't have to kill fuzzy little animals."

"We're Pro-Life now," Sheez said.

Tacks pointed at their clothing. "But you're wearing the furs of animals that died to make your clothes."

Sheez looked down at herself.

The cavemen looked too, purely in the interest of being polite.

"Um, you're right," she said after a moment of consideration. "I didn't think of that."

She looked up and flashed that smile again. "Never mind, we're Pro-Death. Continue with your hunting. We approve."

With that, she whirled, long hair flying, and swung back the direction they had come. The other girls followed, their female body parts moving in the seductive way female body parts were designed to move.

199

The guys admired the view until the girls were out of sight. Then a few seconds longer until the imprinted memory faded.

"Um, where were we?" Wug asked weakly.

"It's time to line them up and march," Lob said. He was the sole caveman not affected by the procession of women.

"Oh, yeah, that's right."

"You also have to assign a general to lead them into battle," Lob said quietly.

Wug looked nervous, "It doesn't have to be me, does it?"

"Of course not," Lob assured him. "Your assistant Berp would do nicely."

Wug looked over at Berp, who had missed the low voiced conversation. "That works for me." He clapped his hands, "All right, men. Attention!"

They all looked at him.

Wug sighed, "Attention means you stand really straight and tall."

"I thought it meant like are we looking at you and listening carefully," Bonk said.

"It does," Wug said. "But it also means the other thing."

"Is this another one of those homo things?" Deth asked.

Area Wug sighed again, wishing he was back in his cave sucking down something naturally fermented. "Yes. Yes, it is. Anyway, in the army, it means get in a line and stand straight."

The cavemen tried.

"We can't," Tacks said. "We're not built that way. We're all hunched over from when we used our arms to walk. We need to do a bit more…" he did finger quotes "…evolving."

"You say that like it's a bad thing," Deth said accusingly.

"It is," Tacks replied. "We're modern cavemen, ya' know."

Wug shook his head and groaned. "Fine, then just stand as straight as you can."

"Hey, wait for me."

They looked up to see Grog rolling his wheel down the path. When he got next to Bonk, he rolled it to a stop, missing Bonk's toes only because Bonk jumped back. "Hey!"

"Oops, sorry," Grog grinned, not looking at all sorry.

"You were just trying to get me back for rolling it over your foot earlier," Bonk accused.

"Nah, it would have been an accident," Grog said with the sincerity of a politician.

"You stole my wheel from me!" Bonk hissed.

Grog's eyes went wide with affected surprise, "What? I bought it from you in a legitimate sales transaction."

"You gave me a rubber check!"

Grog scratched his nose, "Actually, I can't remember if that leaf was from a rubber tree or not."

"It didn't clear the bank," Bonk said. "I put it on the bank, and it bounced."

"Well, rubber is prone to that. You should have known. Seller beware, you know," Grog said.

"I want my wheel back," Bonk said, trying to use the tone of voice Hedz used whenever she scared the heck out of him. He reached for the wheel.

Grog stepped between Bonk and the wheel. "No."

Bonk leveled his spear and growled, "Now."

Grog rolled his eyes. "You're not going to stab me. Besides, did you redeposit the check?"

"Redeposit?"

Grog sighed. "Do I have to explain everything? All you have to do is redeposit the check."

"What's that?"

"You take it to the bank a second time, and this time it's good."

Bonk's fury collapsed in confusion. He was totally unfamiliar with high finance and didn't even know where the check had gone. Was it still at the bank? He would have to go look.

Grog looked at the spear pointed at his gut. "Now will you put that thing away before you hurt yourself?"

"Shut up," Bonk said, lowering the spear.

(note: this is the first recorded evidence of the phrase 'shut up' which would, in time, become the third most used phrase in human existence, right ahead of, 'are we there yet?')

Wug had been watching with the 'I-hope-this-breaks-out-into-a-fight' look, and when a fight didn't materialize, moved quickly to take command of the situation.

"Welcome, Grog," he said. "What's that thing?"

Grinning, Grog gestured to the wheel. "I call it the 'wheel.' It's only known purpose is defense."

"I called it the wheel," Bonk muttered.

"But I bought it from you, so the naming was transferred to me along with the title," Grog said.

Wug looked the wheel over with interest, "Defense, huh? Is it a weapon of mass destruction?"

Grog hesitated for just a moment. "Yep, it is."

Wug looked impressed, "Wow. I can't wait to see that baby in action. Only I won't."

"Why's that?" Droog asked. He was dressed similar to Bonk, with a couple added chevrons on his shoulder that looked like happy faces.

"Because I will not be your field commander," Wug said.

Droog squinted. "Why not?"

"As your leader, it's important that I lead from behind. You can't afford for me to get hurt."

"Um," Bonk started to object.

"So I've appointed a General to lead you in actual combat."

"Who?" Droog shot.

"Berp, of course. He's my most capable lieutenant," Wug said.

"Hey!" Berp cried.

"I thought you said General," Bonk said.

Area Wug shrugged his massive shoulders, displacing a fair amount of air. "General, lieutenant, what's the difference? We haven't invented rank yet."

"I don't want to lead in battle," Berp whimpered.

"Too bad," Wug said.

Berp glared at Lob, standing behind the Chief, "Why not have your new little toady do it?"

Lob quickly slipped a dead rabbit into Wug's hand where it magically disappeared.

"No can do," Wug said. "He's needed here for important war matters."

Berp crossed his arms, "Forget it. I'm not going to support your little war."

Wug's eyebrows jumped. "If you don't support the war it means you don't support the troops."

"You don't support us?" Deth asked Berp.

Berp's head whipped around. "Of course I support you. Just because I don't support the war doesn't mean I don't support my friends."

"We need ya, man," Bonk said. "You're the closest thing to a leader we'll have."

The other cavemen all nodded gravely.

This shocked Berp. He knew the source of his power was always because he sucked up to Area Wug, the biggest caveman in the village. It had never occurred to him that the cavemen actually respected his leadership abilities.

"You're the guy who picked out this area to live," Bonk reminded him.

Berp had nearly forgotten that. A long time ago he had convinced everyone to take up permanent homes in caves rather than wandering around as homeless nomads.

"And you started the Portsbar," Dork said. An important bit of pre-history.

"And remember that time you broke up Deth and Tacks' feud? They would have killed each other if you hadn't stepped in," Droog said.

Deth and Tacks both nodded, and then wacked each other politely on the shoulders with blows the Rock would have been proud of.

Berp was absolutely stunned at this show of support. His head whirling with emotions and thoughts, he jerked his receding chin in acknowledgment. "Okay, fine. I will lead us into battle."

Then he looked up at Wug, and with authority he'd never used before in Wug's presence, he declared, "But I'm going to lead it my way. My decisions are final. We will keep casualties to an absolute minimum."

Wug had been startled by the exchange, too. They respected Berp? The little rodent-faced caveman was, well, maybe not liked, but admired?

He shook off the thought for later consideration. He'd get Lob's opinion on it later. Plus Lob would pay to give his opinion. He'd never eaten this well before with so little effort.

He raised his voice, addressing the troops. "All right, men. Now here's your mission. The Meefs are the cause of all evil! They bring bad weather on us. They hoard all wealth and are the cause of our economic collapse."

"Economic collapse?" Droog whispered to Bonk who shrugged.

"The Meefs are planning our ultimate destruction," Wug thundered. "And they will rain annihilation on us... unless we

204

get them first! We must eradicate them, or put them in camps, where we will be safe from their, uh, … Meefdom."

"Meefdom?" the cavemen all thought.

"You must protect your women! You must protect your leaders! You must protect me!"

The cavemen thought about the comely young women who had just left and shouted, "Yeah!"

"So follow your brave general and bring back their heads!"

"Yeah!" the cavemen shouted. They would have leaped to their feet had they not already been standing.

Berp backed a couple strides until he was on the path. "About face!"

The cavemen rubbed their faces.

"That means turn around," Berp added helpfully.

"Oh," they responded, and turned facing towards the Meef lands.

"Forward, march," Berp commanded, and he started down the path.

"Is there such a thing as a 'backward march'?" Droog whispered to Bonk with a grin on his face.

"How about a 'sideways march'?" Bonk whispered back.

"Or April and March?" Droog quipped.

They disappeared around the bend accompanied by an ominous sound of thunder. Bonk looked over his shoulder, but the sky was clear and bright.

He shrugged, and hurried to keep up.

Chapter 43

Hedz and Lump were doing a bit of fire maintenance, brushing away spent ashes, pushing half burnt twigs back into the fire.

Lump picked up a branch. "So many things have changed since my day."

Hedz nodded politely.

The old woman continued, "Clothes, advanced weaponry, tools. We didn't have all that in my day." Then she pointed at Hedz's cleavage, "And we didn't have that around in my day either."

She looked down at her shrunken chest, "Too bad. I could have used it."

Hedz chuckled.

After a moment, Lump continued. "Do you know why I was already in this cave when you and Bonk first moved in?"

Hedz looked up and locked brown eyes with Lump's watery blue eyes. Strange, she'd never noticed her peculiar eye color.

"They left me here," Lump said flatly.

"Who left you here?" Hedz asked, already knowing the answer.

"My family. We were wanderers. When I got … old … I couldn't keep up. So they left me with just enough food to last until they could get out of sight. Like I'd get to eating and not notice them leave."

Her gaze was steady and not self-pitying. "They left me here to die."

206

Hedz didn't know what to say to that.

"Then you and Bonk moved here," Hedz continued. "And you accepted me, as I am. You took care of me, and made me part of your family."

What could one say to that?

"I never thanked you," Lump said. "I hope that in my own way you understand how I appreciate everything you and Bonk have done for me."

Hedz felt tears rush to her eyes. She leaned over and hugged the old woman. Lump hugged back with fragile strength.

"You are part of our family now," Hedz breathed into Lump's hair.

She pulled away, and saw tears rolling down Lump's weathered old face.

They smiled at each other.

After a few more sentimental moments, which comes more naturally to women, Hedz asked curiously, "What made you tell me that just now?"

"That little guy. Lob?"

Hedz was surprised at the quick change of topic.

"I don't trust him," Lump said. "He reminds me too much of some of the horrible people we had in my tribe. They don't care about life. About people. Not like you do."

"I don't trust him either." Hedz was glad someone shared her feeling.

"I'm afraid of what he might be getting Bonk into," Lump said. "I think you need to leave Eff with me, and go watch after him."

"But I'm just a woman," Hedz said. "How can I protect a big, strong caveman?"

Lump raised a gray eyebrow.

Hedz laughed, "Okay, Bonk's not so strong. But he's big enough to watch over himself."

Lump's eyebrow went up another fraction.

Hedz laughed again, "Right. He needs watching over."

Her smile faded."So you think they're in trouble?"

"I think that Lob guy will do whatever he can to gain power. And if getting rid of other cavemen just to reduce the number of able-bodied men helps him gain power, he will do it."

"You think that's what he's trying to do?"

"I don't know," Lump said. "We may never know his true agenda. But you met these Meefs. Do you think they're really planning on invading us?"

Hedz thought back to her meeting with Cheef and Deef. They had seemed to be very peaceful creatures. Not warlike at all. She shook her head.

"Then you need to make sure nothing happens, to your man, or to those little creatures," Lump said.

Hedz nodded slowly.

"Take the boys with you," Lump said. "They're nearly men now."

Hedz thought about that. Another bit of truth that she hadn't really noticed.

"The baby will be safe with me," Lump assured her.

Chapter 44

Berp marched up the path, or down the path, depending on one's feeling on direction. Behind him, the other cavemen shambled, their neat formation gone amoeba. Rather than marching, they lurched along, long arms easily reaching past their knees. Grog struggled alongside, pushing his wheel over ruts and ignoring Bonk's dark looks. They were no longer far-ranging nomads used to traveling long distances with their entire families. They had founded their little community where river and sea met land, where game was plentiful and nuts, berries and roots grew with no effort on their own.

So they were no longer in shape for long travels, or even the relatively short trip to their neighbors the Meefs. As they walked along, a caveman would drop a hand and knuckle a few steps to relieve the leg strain. The other cavemen were too tired to mock them for monkeying around.

Berp kept the volcano in sight, using it to navigate. He knew he had to be careful because, as a guy, he couldn't ask directions.

The volcano looked different today, its black smoke thicker. But perhaps it was an illusion because they were getting closer. Their path would take them past the volcano and through a long valley. The volcano squatted at the end of the ridge as if guarding the path.

As they walked by the steep rise leading to the volcano's smoking lip, cavemen looked up curiously at the behemoth belching smoke overhead. They were used to seeing it from a distance, but its gaseous output seemed so wispy and inconsequential from their village. Berp wondered the volcano itself wasn't a worthy object to worship. At least no wolverine could eat it. He resolved to think about it.

The valley had been carved out of the ground long ago by retreating glaciers. The Meefs' treetop village lay at the end of the valley. The valley's walls were sheer drops created during the rainy season when the valley would flood with raging currents swollen from runoff from the mountain range up river.

As they walked further into the valley, Berp studied the walls, worried the Meefs might somehow climb and rain rocks and boulders on their heads. He motioned his men to move closer to the center of the gully.

Droog pointed at a smudge of green at the end of the valley whose color stood out among the reddish brown earthen walls towering around them. "I think that's it."

"Yeah," Bonk said, his eyes roving. He felt a strange unease in this quiet place. There was no wildlife in sight. No birds flitting from branch to branch. No sharp barks from foxes as they chased small critters through the tall grasses. No plant life dared life in this place.

He could see gullies carved into the side of the valley and imagined water rushing through them making the valley a kill-zone. With a bit of effort, someone might be able to climb, but it would not be an easy trip, and it would be impossible if waters were racing down.

Grog wheeled his wheel, thinking how it would roll if pushed down these steep walls. He remembered his wild ride atop the wheel and shivered.

Deth and Tacks cast uneasy glances around, and gripped their spears more tightly. Nature's immenseness intimidated them far more than any live creature could. Except mastodons. Those guys were pretty scary. And the dire wolves. Nasty creatures. And saber-tooth cats. You don't want to mess with their huge fangs. And who would want to tangle with a salt water croc. And the giant sloth. What a … Okay, okay, they were just as intimidated by live creatures as they were by the landscape. Still, though, this landscape was scary. This made them respect the Meefs, who lived near this desolation every day. Each of them missed their green little slice of paradise. Traveling makes you appreciate your home all the more. And these former nomads were appreciating their little caves right then.

As they came nearer to the green making up the Meef's homes, they started shaking the foreboding that had crept over them in the desolate valley. They could pick out individual trees now, and the forbidding volcano became a casualty to distance.

"I didn't like that place," Bonk said.

It was the first time anyone had said anything in awhile.

"Yeah, kind of creepy," Droog agreed. "I think if we had gone on top of the ridge, I'd have felt better."

Bonk looked up at the ledge overhead. "Yeah. Maybe there's a path up there."

Droog sighed, "At least we didn't have to climb. I guess I understand why we went this way. And maybe militarily it made more sense. But what do I know? I'm just a grunt."

As they got closer to the Meef village, the cavemen's spirits and hubris picked up more, and they were once again starting to feel invincible. Each of the cavemen looked at his fellows, large muscular cavemen with long muscled arms, big heavy callused feet, and heads harder and stronger than an NFL helmet, and they felt the power of their combined might. They were armed with the latest technologically advanced spears ever made, the stones chipped to a killing sharpness.

The Meefs were charred henge.

Chapter 45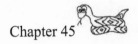

Along the top of the ridge. Bush kneeled a few feet from the edge, dangling the snake over the edge. The snake was pooping frantically.

"Do you see anything, boy?" Bush asked.

Frigg scooted a bit closer. "How do you know he's a boy snake? They don't exactly have boy and girl parts."

Bush threw an irritated look over his shoulder. "Duh, he's mine, right? If I was a girl, he would be a girl snake."

Frigg couldn't quite pick out the illogic of this, so he didn't say anything.

"Boys," Hedz whispered. "We can see them from here." She was peering over a large rock at the valley below.

Keeping low, Frigg and Bush scurried over to her.

They could see the cavemen, small dots from this distance, moving steadily towards the end of the valley.

"How come we can't let them see us?" Frigg asked.

"They'd send us home," Hedz replied.

"But they're grown men," Bush said. "What can we do to protect them?"

Hedz brushed a stray strand of hair from her face. "I don't know. But I just have the feeling we should be here."

"Works for me," Frigg said.

Then they heard a scrabbling behind some boulders. They stiffened.

A furry head peeked over and a squeaky voice said, "Whys are your mensfolk our village coming?"

Bush whipped his walking stick around and brandished the snake.

The snake flicked its tongue and the Meefs froze.

"Cheef," Hedz said.

The first one looked up sharply at its name.

"Deef," Hedz named the other one.

"That's us," Deef acknowledged. "Whys are you and your mensfolk here?"

Hedz wasn't sure how to answer this. Neither of the Meefs appeared to be armed, and they were small creatures, dwarfed even by young not-quite cavemen Frigg and Bush. Their claws, though, were wickedly sharp and would no doubt be effective weapons.

Cheef peered over the edge at the cavemen advancing on their homestead. "We's watchings your mensfolk. Tries to understands."

"Yours people look not happy to come to our home," Deef added.

Hedz took a deep breath. This was why she was here, to perhaps prevent something that shouldn't happen. What she did next might have profound consequences for either or both tribes.

Finally she took the plunge and in a quiet voice said, "Our men are coming to attack your village."

The two squirrels jumped.

"Comings to hurt us?" Deef squeaked.

"But why?" Cheef 's eyes were wide with fright. He clenched his clever fingers, and Hedz backed up a step from the needle-like claws.

"Because we've been told that you have been preparing to attack us."

The two Meefs glanced at each other and then back at her, "We's not attack anyones," Cheef said.

213

"Then why have you been preparing weapons of mass destruction?"

The Meefs exchanged another look of complete bafflement.

"We's not makings weapons," Cheef declared. "We's friendly. We's don't fight. We run."

"And climb," Deef added.

"Right," Cheef said. "Whens there's trouble, we make sures we aren't where troubles is."

"Lots of thingsees likes to eats Meefs," Deef said gravely.

Suddenly Hedz understood. For some reason known only to him, Lob had convinced the tribe that the Meefs were a threat, and now the two tribes were on the brink of a very bloody battle. They had to get down and warn the cavemen that it was all a mistake.

And that's when something massive roared.

Chapter 46

The cavemen looked at the trees towering overhead.

"Look around for water," Berp instructed. "And someone remind me next time to bring canteens."

"What's a canteen?" Bonk asked.

"It's a vessel for carrying water. We haven't invented it yet," Dork said.

"Well okay, then," Bonk said. "We'll bring shells or something."

"Now where are those Meefs?" Berp looked up into the trees. There were vines and intricate walkways linking trees together, but no sign of the critters who lived there.

They ventured cautiously into the woods, eyes alert for objects tossed down from the trees.

"Watch for pits," Berp said. They were well aware of pit traps, something they used themselves to bring down large game. To the small squirrel creatures, the cavemen could be seen as large predators.

"Look," Deth suddenly cried.

They followed his pointing finger, and they saw it, too. A gray shape flitting from a tree to a cylindrical structure high up in the trees. Then it peeked around the structure at them.

"We see you," Deth shouted. "We know you're up there!" Silence.

Finally, a Meef came out, and holding onto vines peered anxiously down at them. Another followed and they perched on a branch.

"Whys are yous here?" the first one squeaked.

"We're here to destroy you," Tacks cried.

"Shhhh," Berp hissed. "I'm in charge. I'll do the speaking." He looked up at the agitated creature perched far above. "He's right, we're here to destroy you."

There was a collective gasp from the leaves above. Now they could see more of the squirrel tribe scattered in the branches, eyes on the army below.

"We's don't wants to be destroyed."

"Too bad," Berp said. "I don't make the rules, you know. So come down here and get destroyed."

Bonk raised a finger, "Actually, Wug said something about putting them into confinement camps, so maybe we don't have to kill them."

"Yeah," Deth said. "We could concentrate them in one place, control them."

"We'll talk about it later," Berp said. He looked up again. "Okay, come on down here."

The air was filled with a strange chittering language as the Meefs talked it over amongst themselves.

Finally, the first one said, "No."

Berp shook with anger, "I said, come down here, coward!"

The squirrel turned to its companion and asked, 'What's coward?"

"I's think it someone who doesn't go unarmed to meet armsed people," the other one responded.

"Oh, so's he's sayings we's smart?" the first one asked.

"Yes," the other said.

"Oh, good." Then he shouted down to Berp, "Thanks for callings me a cowards. Verys nice of you."

"It's not a compliment," Berp started to say, and then he frowned. The tree next to him was starting to vibrate. He looked up. Nothing was up the tree.

The vibration also had gotten the Meef's attention. The first one looked into the distant horizon and studied it. Then it

216

turned back to the cavemen below. "I's very pleased to meets yous, but yous need to goes back to yours owns homes now."

"There's no way…" Berp started to say.

But then he felt a vibration in the ground and heard a distant rumbling. He whirled and looked at the volcano. It was belching smoke, but didn't appear to be the source of the shaking ground. Another earth moving?

The Meef whistled. When it had Berp's attention it pointed to the wide prairie abutting the small forest. A long line of black stretched from one side of the plain to the other. Tan dust swirled overhead, casting the line in even more shadow. A herd of excited bison was thundering at them. And closing rapidly.

"Stampedes coming," the Meef pointed out. It whistled to the other Meefs, and they started moving through the trees to a safer location.

Berp's eyes widened. "Retreat!"

"What's that?" Bonk asked.

"It means run away," Berp said, and he personally showed his men how it was done.

They fled back down the valley toward home, a million bison bearing down on them.

Chapter 47

Giant sloth!

Hedz screamed. Frigg and Bush screamed. The Meefs screamed.

Some or all of them might have squirted a bit of pee.

The huge shaggy beast roared again, and stepped around the rocks.

"Theys eats us," Cheef cried. The sloth was between them and their home, so he grabbed his mate's furry paw, and they started running along the ledge in the opposite direction.

Hedz, Frigg and Bush were on their heels.

The sloth glared at them with angry reddened eyes, and took off in pursuit. Definitely not a vegetarian.

....

Bonk raced after Berp, his forgotten spear clattering to the ground. The spear wouldn't be a deterrent to a herd of bison. The other cavemen strung out behind them, followed by Grog, wheeling his wheel as fast as he could.

Tacks raced by Grog. "Get rid of that thing."

"Can't," Grog gasped, pushing with all his might. "This might be the only weapon that can save us."

Tacks just shook his head, and bolted after the other cavemen, who seemed to have forgotten their fatigue.

As the thundering herd got closer, the ground became less stable, making footing treacherous and uncertain. The cavemen ran, knowing that only death met them if the herd caught up with them.

....

Above, the gigantic sloth chased five humanoid figures. The sloth's apparent slow-motion movements were deceptive because its huge stride covered yards at a time. It was keeping pace with its prey.

Hedz and the boys blindly followed the Meefs, relying on them to know the terrain. At the same time, she feared they might lead her to their people, which would be more trouble. But she preferred taking that risk to getting sliced and diced by the sloth's scythe-like talons.

Frigg stumbled over the uneven ground. "I'm scared."

"Me, too," Bush said, stubbornly maintaining his grip on his stick. He was holding the walking stick facing the wrong way, so the snake was looking backwards over Bush's shoulder. And what it saw lumbering after them was making the snake poop in fright.

....

Down in the valley, the cavemen were in a panicked sprint from the bison who had just thundered into the valley, their hooves echoing in the tunnel-like valley. Soon the cavemen dropped to all fours, knuckling through the rocks as the ground shuddered.

They raced under the shadow of the huge volcano which ignored the drama unfolding beneath it, because it was busy dealing with its own internal drama.

Chapter 48

Hedz, the boys and the Meefs ran along the side of the volcano, the sloth hot on their heels. The sides of the volcano shuddered from some inner turmoil developing far underground.

Suddenly the Meefs disappeared.

Hedz looked around frantically. Where'd they go?

The ground thumped from the impact of the sloth's massive frame, which was a fragile touch compared to what was going on underground.

A sharp whistle. One of the Meefs gestured from a narrow ravine that had been created by water runoff.

Hedz grabbed the boys, and shoved them down the ravine, praying it would be too tight of a squeeze for the monster chasing after them.

As they slid down the ravine, she heard the sloth growl and shove its massive body into the ravine.

Ahead, the Meefs clambered over the rocks with squirrel-like speed and agility. She and the boys followed with less agility but plenty of motivation furnished by the sloth thundering after them with no agility but plenty of power.

Then the sloth's forward progress stopped.

It had gotten wedged into the ravine. Roaring in fury and panic, the sloth slashed with great sweeping claws at the unyielding earth.

Hedz, the boys and the Meefs scurried away as fast as they could, trying to ignore the ground-shaking havoc.

Chapter 49

Bonk looked over his shoulder and his heart sank. "We aren't going to make it."

Droog shot a glance back and saw huge, fearsome bison, horned heads four feet wide. They were so close now he could see their maddened red eyes and foamed flecked mouths dripping stringy bits of saliva. They were oblivious to anything they might stomp beneath their massive hooves and would run until either exhaustion or death took them.

Droog's face paled. "I don't want to die like this."

Then he saw what had started the stampede. Great tawny shapes were bounding along the tapering walls of the embankment. A pride of lions, trying to pick out the young and weak.

So the cavemen's choice was to die under the hooves of the bison, or the claws of the enormous cats.

"Hsssss!"

"Did you spring a leak?" Bonk asked.

"What?"

Then Bonk saw a slim brown arm beckoning from the wall just ahead. The arm was followed by a head, with a great wonderful flowing mustache.

"Bonk!"

"Hedz?"

"Quick, get in here," she cried. She was in one of the ravines rippling the walls of the valley.

Bonk glanced at the cavemen behind him. He may have been a bad hunter, but he was an excellent runner, so they were trailing. "Hey, guys, this way."

Totally exhausted, the army of cavemen had nearly been ready to concede their lives to the rampaging herd. But when they saw a possible escape, hope gave them fresh legs.

Bonk dived into the ravine, where he found not only his mate, but Frigg and Bush.

Behind the boys, steam poured from a vent-like tunnel carved into the rock.

"Get in here," Hedz said, leading him into the tunnel which was considerably warmer than most caves he'd been in. And as a caveman, he had fair bit of experience with caves.

As he followed her dark form into the shadows he could see she was following someone else. A couple someones. Meefs?

Meanwhile, the cavemen climbed in behind him, puffing and grunting. Too panicked to look around, they popped into the cave with the alacrity of Bonk-a-Moles.

Behind them, Grog doggedly rolled his wheel along. He wheeled it up the incline, panting with the exertion. Then there was a guttural roar behind him. He turned to see a great female lion bounding toward him. He quickly shoved the wheel into place at the mouth of the cave and slid by. He let it fall, perfectly sealing the mouth of the cave.

The lion skidded to a halt, and pawed at the wheel, sensing easy prey inside. Prey that didn't have horn and hooves. It clawed at the wheel, the rasping sounds audible to Grog cowering on the inside and praying to the Dead Platypus God.

God must have heard his prayers, because after a last frustrated snarl, the lioness took off to resume its chase of the fleeing bison.

That's when the volcano blew.

....

Nestled high in pines on a small rocky hill, the Meef tribe watched millions of bison surge through the forest, trampling underbrush, their maddened rush taking down fully grown trees. The Meefs could only watch sadly as their tree-top village disappeared under massive hooves.

Chapter 50

Back at the caveman village, Area Wug had convened a council with Lob, and they were dining on freshly caught gophers. As Wug munched a plump gopher leg, he marveled at what a prolific hunter Lob was. Lob was always there, ready and able to provide fish, rabbit or squirrel. Wug opened his mouth to compliment Lob when he happened to look towards the hills just in time to see the conical top of the volcano explode with a thunderous, ground-shaking detonation. The massive explosion violently ejected millions of tons of cinder and ash, sending a tremendous shock wave down the entire valley that would have broken every window in the village had there been any windows in the village to break.

Chapter 51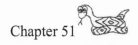

Meanwhile, inside the volcano the ground was heaving and shaking, jostling its occupants like human-sized playing dice. Cheef and Deef knew exactly what was going on. Living next to the volcano their entire lives, they had learned to interpret its moods and actions. And now they knew they shouldn't be where they were.

They rushed back towards the opening of the small cave, pushing past surprised cavemen.

"We's must leaves," Cheef cried.

"What are you talking about?" Hedz's arms were planted against the walls to keep from being thrown off her feet.

"And what are you doing here?" Berp asked over the sonic booms reverberating through the cave. He had just noticed the Meefs and Bonk's family.

"Nos times for that's," Deef said, shoving through furry caveman legs as she struggled to catch up with her mate.

"We's must leaves," Cheef repeated. The mouth of the tunnel was blocked by the wheel. "Nooo!" he squeaked, eyes bright with alarm.

"What's the problem?" Grog was slumped against the wall.

Cheef pointed back into the cave. "Eets dangerous. Gases that kills Meefs."

Berp snorted. "Ah, so finally we get the truth. Weapons of mass destruction, eh?"

Deef frowned. "Weapons? We's don't know. Destruction. Yess. We's must leaves." She looked with alarm back into the

225

cave. The tunnel was a natural fissure vent created by escaping gases.

Caught up in the Meefs' urgency, Hedz shoved past cavemen. The wheel was perfectly aligned with the mouth of the cave. "Get this out of here."

Grog looked up, his eyes exhausted. "What?"

"If you don't move this, we die," she growled.

Grog immediately forgot his fatigue, and shoved the big wheel aside.

The Meefs scampered outside, and looked around.

The side of the mountain was sliding down towards them. Urgently they gestured to the cavemen. "Comes. You musts comes."

"Bonk, boys, go," Hedz said. When they hesitated, she said, "Now!" Her eyes swept the rest of the cavemen huddled inside. "You, too. Everyone. Get out."

The cavemen streamed out of the cave into a dark hell. The sky was gone, replaced by smoke and volcanic debris shooting into the air. There was no sign of the lions, but below them the tremendous herd had paused in its headlong rush down the valley. There are very few things that will stop bison stampede in its tracks, and an exploding volcano was one of those things.

An onrushing flood of lahar the consistency of wet cement gushed out of the side of the volcano and the pyroclastic material, rocks and water were flooding the valley, splitting the massive herd into two parts. The buffalo that had already passed the volcano galloped ever more furiously towards the village. But that was the small part of the mega herd. The millions more that had been following were now milling around, building momentum the opposite direction, back where they had come. They mindlessly trampled over any of their number too slow to react. Any buffalo left behind got swept into the mud and lava flow.

226

Meanwhile, a hissing sound escaped the fissure vent and Cheef's eyes widened.

"We's must go. We's must go."

He and Deef ran down the side of the volcano in the direction of Bonk's village.

The cavemen didn't need any more urging, and quickly followed the Meefs. As they reached the floor of the valley, a gigantic blast of sulfur and poisonous gases erupted from the fissure. They didn't notice because they were too busy fleeing the massive mudflow systematically swallowing the valley.

"Aaaeeeee!" They raced ahead of the mud, charred bits of flaming debris showering down on them.

Fortunately the valley was wide enough to slow the steaming lahar flow and they were able to keep just ahead of it.

But right on their heels was the giant sloth which had somehow freed itself. It was hard to tell if the leviathan was chasing them or fleeing the lahar flow.

Fortunately, the herd of buffalo had trampled the ground nice and flat.

Unfortunately, there were piles of slippery squashed buffalo dung all around.

Fortunately, they were already scared, so the fear of the sloth didn't add all that much to their level of scaredness.

Unfortunately, they were already tired.

Fortunately, they were scared enough for that not to be much of a problem.

Chapter 52

The ground shook like a rat in a terrier's grip. With baby Eff nestled securely under her arm, Lump poked a head out of the cave.

Gop looked at the dark sky. "What is it?" Bits of flaming cinder rained down and they hastily pulled their heads back into the cave.

"It's an eruption," Lump said. She'd lived there long enough to recognize that this was a result of the volcano. It had never acted up this much before though.

Suddenly a torrent of dirt thumped onto the ground in front of the cave mouth, caused by an avalanche of dirt dislodged from uphill.

The dust and soot drove them deeper into the cave.

Chapter 53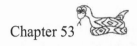

Area Wug calmly watched the cataclysm going on all around him. "I gotta admit, Lob. When you do something, you do it big. How did you arrange all this?" He gestured at the smoke, the dark, ashes and gunk raining down from the sky, the ground shaking and thousands of buffalo blindly thundering past, followed closely by a huge pride of lions.

Lob's mouth was open. He was in too much shock to try and invent a story that would allow him to take credit for everything going on around them.

Then they heard something kind of whiny. It sounded a bit like, "Aaaaiiiiieeeeee."

They looked up the valley pass and racing behind the buffalo was the caveman army, with two small critters scampering ahead. Behind them was a leviathan sloth, and behind it, dwarfing the sloth, was a wall of rolling mud, thirty feet high.

Wug chuckled. "Seriously, Lob. This is, like, over the top. I'm going to have to make you my Minister of Special Effects, because this is just too cool."

When Lob saw the mud coming at him, his agile-though-evil-mind quickly did some calculations.

Then Wug noticed the small running creatures, "Hey, are those Meefs?"

Lob didn't answer.

Mostly because he was sprinting away.

Wug watched him go, his mouth open and full of tender gopher nuggets.

The caveman army, hoarse from screaming, and running on all fours, stumbled into the village tripping over their long hair. They immediately made for their caves on higher ground. Meanwhile, the shuddering ground was convincing the higher ground to try to become lower ground, so the cavemen found themselves stumbling over sheets of dirt and rolling debris.

Meanwhile, the immense wall of mud headed straight for low ground, that being the river. Millions of tons of volcano barf plunged into the river, dislodging hundreds of salt water crocodiles. They tried to flee upriver but found their path blocked by a jutting plate of earth which had shifted from quakes triggered by the volcano's ferocity. With nowhere to go, the crocs erupted from the water, running as fast as their short stubby legs would allow. They were heading in the same direction Lob had gone.

The humongous sloth staggered into the village.

Then it saw Area Wug. No one knew what the sloth was thinking, but when it saw the huge hairy caveman, its small eyes widened, and it lumbered at him.

Wug tried to shriek, but his mouth was full of gopher, so he spit it out, and tried again. This time he was rewarded by the same beautiful E note that had first prompted him to try to start a rock band.

The sloth seemed to like it, too, and roared back a perfectly executed F note. Then it reared, which has nothing to do with its butt, opening its arms wide. No one will know if it meant to grab him, hug him or squash him, because Wug wasn't there when the arms converged on where he used to be.

Instead, he was running after the crocodiles,

  … which were running after Lob

    … who was running after the lions

      … which were running after the buffalo

       …who were just running because of their herd mentality.

The sloth was exhausted, and perhaps because of this it wasn't thinking clearly. So just reacting, it joined the chase.

"C'mon," Hedz said to the Meefs, gesturing to the cave. The entrance was barricaded with dirt, but Bonk, Hedz, Frigg and Bush pushed their way inside. The Meefs hesitated, looked around at the mayhem and cast a long longing look at the horizon where their village was hidden by distance. Then they dived into the cave.

Chapter 54

Lob was livid.

He loped along, dodging buffalo chips, keeping a wary eye out for the lions.

He'd almost had everything set up. He would have been in control. Life would have been so easy. No more frantic hunting to come up with bribes. Taxation would have given him everything he needed in life. He would have his pick of young nubile cave girls.

Perhaps Sheez. Maybe Gop. Or both. A harem.

Yes, he would have had a harem.

And then it had all come crashing down. He knew the mudslide would change both the physical and political landscape, affecting hunting and forcing them to rebuild. He didn't want to rebuild. He wanted to rule, even if through an idiot like Area Wug. Jeesh, he's never met such a malleable person before. Or one so susceptible to greed and manipulation. In other words, the perfect politician for someone like Lob.

"Grrr."

Lob paused. He had been 'grrrr'ing' in his mind, but hadn't really planned on 'grrrr'ing' out loud. So maybe it wasn't him that 'grrrr'd."

He looked around, and then he saw the lioness.

"AAAeeeeeeiiiiiieeee!"

He whirled, and headed the other direction.

The lion rumbled a warning, but didn't chase him. She had just been protecting her kill, a buffalo calf she had separated from the herd.

Lob didn't know that, so he was running full out.

"Grrrrr."

He hadn't done that 'grrrr' either. In fact, he wasn't feeling very 'grrrrr-like' at all anymore. More like 'aaiiieeee-like.'

The ground was moving at him. How could ground move?

Then he realized. It wasn't the ground moving. It was hundreds of crocodiles running up the path directly at him. Huge goliath crocs, thirty feet and more, smaller ones, young crocs, a moving carpet of scales, tails and teeth.

Lob shrieked, and ran in the only other direction available. Towards the tar pits.

That Big Stinky Place.

As Lob fled down the ravine leading to the tar pits, the crocs followed, mostly because it was downhill and easier going for short-legged reptiles.

Behind the crocs, Area Wug sprinted down the path the other direction, his E note melding in perfect harmony with the F note roaring of the sloth lumbering after him.

As Lob neared the tar pit, he skidded to a halt, nearly tumbling into the thick viscous gunk. Behind him the steady thumping of webbed crocodile feet rustled through the underbrush.

Lob headed around the tar pits, his destination a small glen in the distance. He'd climb a tree and wait for the reptiles to return to their water.

Suddenly there was a piecing shriek and claws clamped onto the small caveman's shoulders. There was a mighty beating of wings, a downdraft of air, and Lob felt himself being lifted into the air.

"Aaaiiieeee!"

He looked up and saw he was in the grasp of a mighty eagle. A bald one. There wasn't a feather on its head.

At another time, the sight of a bald eagle might have been amusing. But not now. Seeing the ground fall away, Lob frantically struggled, swinging his fists, trying to punch the eagle. Fortunately, his arms were caveman-length and he managed to grab a fist-full of feathers. The eagle shrieked, buffeting Lob with mighty blows from its wings. Lob grabbed and clawed, tearing feathers loose. Finally, with a cry of anger, the eagle released him.

As Lob fell, his agile mind realized he would not be injured by the fall. They were not high enough yet. There was just enough time for him to think he would never forget this day.

To better keep his balance upon landing, he let go of the feathers.

Seconds later, he hit ground. A soft landing, way softer than he had expected.

Even better, he landed on his feet, sticking the landing perfectly like a gymnast.

But when he tried unsticking the landing, he found he couldn't.

And he never would.

He was stuck in the middle of the tar pit.

He tried to pull his leg up and lost his balance, falling face first into the hot muck. Somehow he made it back to his feet, and looked down. He was covered with black tar. Then the eagle feathers that had been floating above him finally caught up and were sucked onto the tar on his face and chest. He tried brushing them off but managed only to spread feathers all over the thick gooey muck.

Suddenly he heard another loud shriek from the bird of prey and the nearly naked eagle swept from the sky and

234

slammed into Lob, knocking him onto his back into the permanent embrace of the bubbling petroleum.

The last thing he saw as he lay on his back in the sticky tar was the nearly featherless eagle winging away into the blue sky. He found himself saluting.

Chapter 55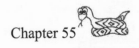

Area Wug realized he'd finally lost the sloth. The sloth's endurance had finally faltered and Wug had steadily gotten further and further ahead of his pursuer.

But the creature was still between him and the village, and he didn't know if it would stay near the path or venture some distance either way from the path. He didn't want to risk running into a rested sloth on the way back, so he decided he would continue on his path and take a circular route back to his village.

He wondered what he would find back in the village. Lob seemed to have deserted, perhaps for good. Berp had been still leading the caveman army, so he would still have his toady. Too bad he wouldn't get any more free treats from Lob. He's put on a bit of a gut with the constant food, obtained without the necessity of him expending time and effort to hunt it himself. Maybe this excursion into unknown territory would do some good, since it would give him a chance to work off some of his newfound chub.

Then he saw something that gave him chills. A man's skull, on a spear.

He froze.

He had fled so far he was now in the lands belonging to one of the most frightening tribes of humans in existence. Cannibals.

They had crossed paths with cannibals during their nomad travels, long ago, when Wug was just a boy. But what he had

seen he had never forgotten. He hadn't realized he had
ventured so far from his village.

He shivered with revulsion, and backed away quietly, right
into something sharp.

A branch?

Or Lob? Maybe Lob came back and had a squirrel on a
stick for him.

Yum.

He turned slowly, and his insides turned to mush.

Chapter 56

The volcano finally finished its temper tantrum. It hadn't been a major eruption. Still though, it had barfed a considerable amount of mud and smoke. Sediment would stain the sky until gravity finally pulled it back to earth. Meanwhile, bits of charcoal and ash danced in the air currents.

The river had barely noticed the mud slide, mindlessly detouring around and eroding the mud, eventually washing the volcano debris into the sea. The crocodiles would come back, forgiving their river like lovers, and soon their little reptile minds will have forgotten all about it.

Bonk was busy digging out the rest of the cave entrance, helped by the Meefs, who flung the dirt between their legs like meerkats.

The fire had somehow been kicked over and trampled into the dirt. Hedz poked through the dust, looking for an ember. After searching for a few moments, Hedz sighed. "I think we lost it."

"We lost the fire?" Gop moaned.

"Don't worry," Hedz said. "The eruption opened a lava spring near our bathroom."

"Bathroom?" Bonk asked.

"You know, where we evacuate our waste?"

"Huh?"

Hedz sighed, "Pee? Poop?"

Bonk's face cleared of confusion. "Oh, why didn't you say that? Heh, and you said 'pee' and 'poop.'"

Hedz just shook her head. "Anyway, the lava springs have different temperatures. Some of them are hot enough to cook meat. Other bits are a bit cooler, perfect for baths."

"Nooooooo! Not baths," Frigg and Bush moaned.

"Yay, baths," Gop clapped.

"I think the baby could use one right now," Lump said, sitting by the entrance with Eff on her lap.

It was the first time Bonk could recall Lump actually leaving the shadows of the cave. He saw a look pass between Hedz and Lump. He shrugged. Women stuff.

He and the Meefs did a final swipe and the cave entrance was cleared.

"Well, thanks, little guys," he said.

"Ours pleasure," Cheef squeaked.

"Can you stick around for dinner?" Bonk asked. They had a huge supply of buffalo meat, much of it cooked and tasty, courtesy of volcano lava. The villagers had been gorging themselves, trying to eat as much as possible before the meat went bad. It was times like this Bonk wished Dork would get around to inventing that refrigeration thing he kept crowing about.

Deef shook her head. "Nos. We don't eats the meats. Nuts and sstuffs. We's likes those."

"But we's thanks," Cheef said. "Ands we's must sees that's our homeses are safe."

"I understand," Bonk replied.

He looked at the two small creatures. He couldn't believe he had ever thought of them as adversaries.

"Friends?" he asked.

The Meefs grinned big rodent smiles. "Friendss,' they chimed.

Then they headed up the hill to take the the ridge path home since the valley was filled with drying, steaming mud.

Bonk was tired, and sat down on the ledge overlooking their valley. While the terrain had shifted a bit due to the natural catastrophe, it was much the same, and would quickly return to normal.

Hedz settled next to him. "Nobody's seen Area Wug. Or that Lob guy."

Bonk nodded. " I gotta tell you. I don't really miss either one of them."

Hedz squeezed his waist. "I think Berp will be a fine leader."

Her caveman sighed. "Yeah, I guess. I think leadership's overrated. As long as people work together, we'll be fine. Still, though, I can't help but wonder where Wug went."

Chapter 57

Area Wug himself would have loved to be around to answer this question. But he couldn't, mostly because he was a bit tied up.

He was laying next to a simmering lava pool, lashed tightly with vines, surrounded by a tribe of hungry looking cavemen, each looking at him with the look of a diner picking out a live lobster for his meal.

"Lots of meat on this one," a cannibal commented.

Wug shrieked. "No! It's all fat. I'm bad for your cholesterol level!"

Another cannibal shook his head. "I dunno. I think there's both good and bad cholesterol."

"There is! I know! But trust me, I'm the bad kind, "Wug cried.

A cannibal grinned with teeth that had never seen floss. "Dibs on a drumstick. I like dark meat."

Wug struggled to hide his big, beefy leg.

Another one looked critically at Wug's mass. "We could feed for weeks on this."

"Yum," another said.

"Mmm-mmm-good," another said.

The head cannibal grinned. "You got that right. Hey, someone go get Campbell."

"Yeah," another cannibal agreed, "Campbell makes the best soup."

"No, I would make horrible soup," Wug cried. "Too much gristle. No flavor."

The cannibal chief shook his head. "I disagree. You will taste just fine."

He gestured. "Go, get Campbell."

One of the cannibals headed uphill to the caves. Soon he was back with another caveman who was carrying a folded leaf and wearing a belt of dried intestines decorated with human femurs.

Campbell took a long assessing look at Wug. "Whoa, he's a big one. Someone go back and get another leaf of flavorings."

A young cannibal immediately bolted up the hill.

Campbell held the leaf over the lava pool, tipping it and spilling herbs and spices onto the bubbling surface.

"Don't do this," Wug pleaded.

Campbell ignored him and pulled a femur from his belt. He swirled the herb mixture into the liquid, releasing a pleasing aroma. Then he dipped a finger in and tasted it. "I was right. It needs a bit more seasoning."

Just then the young cannibal returned with another folded leaf. Campbell dumped the contents in and inhaled the fumes.

"Ah, perfect." He gestured to the trussed up victim. "Time for the main ingredient."

"No, don't!" Wug wailed.

Three cannibals gave him a shove, and he toppled into the water.

...

Though some people cringe at the evilness of cannibalism, one thing could be said for this particular tribe.

They weren't wasteful.

For in death Area Wug fulfilled a much more serviceable function. Well, his large furry hide did ... stretched out as a carpet for a family of cannibals.

242

Chapter 58

As Bonk, Hedz and family slumbered, and unseen by
Lump monitoring the fire, Sssss felt the cord binding it begin to
relax. The small serpent flexed its muscles, releasing the stick
that had been loosely sticking out of its back. It wriggled out of
the binding and paused, enjoying the warmth of the fire. Then
it flicked a tongue towards the old lady tending the fire, and
sensing no threat, crawled towards the sleeping pit. For a long
moment, it gazed down at the boy who had lashed it to a stick.
No one knew what the snake was thinking, what it was feeling.
Perhaps nothing, perhaps mixed anger and gratitude for its
maiming but subsequent adventures. Other than a healed scar,
the snake felt normal.

After another few moments, Sssss slithered without notice
past the old lady into the darkness to go look for a mouse or
something.

Epilogue

A long time later, a few hundred thousand years, give or take a few hundred thousand years - but who's counting - a young anthropologist internist named Wylie Butts, a graduate student from the University of Chicago, was digging in the tar pits and found something that first puzzled him.

He dug some more and the more he unearthed, the more puzzled he became.

It couldn't be?

This was like no species of animal he'd ever seen.

Surely it was a hoax.

But no, the tar had done a superb job protecting the integrity of the bones and their placement. Besides, they fit too well together.

He looked around cautiously, wondering if it was an elaborate prank by a fellow anthropologist. But, no, it wasn't. He had stumbled across a previously undiscovered species.

A skeleton with parts from a hyena, snake and weasel ... covered in feathers.

Acknowledgments

I want to thank my advance readers, an eclectic and fun bunch. Even better is how I 'met' all of them.

Amana Sebastian is a cool Canadian 'friended' on Myspace because she was a fan of humor (or as she would write, 'humour'). She once sent me a picture of her bookcase to show my books sitting with more highfalutin works. Looked a bit like Bugs Bunny in a Harvard Law class picture.

Taren Wilson, a schoolteacher who out of the blue took me up on a Twitter offer.

Kurt Preston, a geologist who travels the US, writing about strange happenings and probably making other strange happenings happen. We met while chatting with Christopher Moore at Anderson's Books. I liked standing next to Kurt because his shirts are even uglier than mine.

Alison Mills, the Oregon Roller Derby Mama from Myspace who got hooked onto my books. And here's something strange but true about Alison - Christopher Moore autographed her leg at a book-signing, then her husband tattooed the signature to her leg. I think this says a lot about both Alison and her husband.

The thing each of these readers has in common is they are intelligent, thoughtful people who appreciate ludicrousness and flare at injustices. I'm honored (or honoured for Amanda) they took the time to read and make some incredible suggestions. Any screw-ups that survived their scrutiny were probably pointed out by them and missed by me in my editing.

Also, thanks to my younger daughter Lauren who guided me through the Photoshop elements that had me pulling out both of my hairs, and to fellow author Kathleen Baldwin who

reached out to do the cover design. Check her out at
www.kathleenbaldwin.com

And I just want to mention here that my older daughter
Sam's cat is a demon. Just saying. And now it's copywritten,
so it must be true.

Following is a preview of WereWoof, a humor YA vampire/werewolf book published in early 2011.

Preview of WereWoof

"C'mon, boy. Fetch!"
The absolute worst thing you could say to a werewolf.

Chapter 1

Beware of Dog.
Someone had crossed 'dog' off the sign, scrawling the word 'wolf' in crude letters. The 'a' was replaced with an 'e,' so the sign now read, "Bewere of Wolf."
Trug ignored the sign and trotted past the dilapidated house guarding the path to the forest.

As he crossed the forest's outermost undergrowth, the temperature dropped and the noise and bustle of civilization grew muted. His sharp ears could still catch the sounds of humanity behind him, but his attention was on the far more interesting noises and movements of the woods.

He left the path and loped through the underbrush, ducking shrubs and leaping over downed trees. The wind whistled by his ears and the pungent smells of the woods brought a rich array of aromas he'd never encountered. Each scent was its own lavish bouquet delivered on an olfactory platter that would put the best restaurants to shame.

A small creek loomed ahead of him and without breaking stride, he effortlessly bounded to the other bank.

He felt so free … so … well… naked …

Then he spied a certain tree that cried 'territorial marker.' He spun to a stop, lifted a leg and shot some liquid on it. My tree.

As he went to resume his romp, something chomped him on the leg. He skidded to a stop and nibbled at the spot. He could smell flea but didn't get the irritating critter.

Then there was a rustle in the leaves. He whipped around and his ears jumped to attention. His nose twitched, trying to pick up scent. Another new thing. He'd never felt his nose twitch, much less been able to see it without crossing his eyes or looking in the mirror. Weird.

Ah, it was just the wind.

An errant leaf fluttered from an oak and reluctantly rode gravity towards the ground. In joyful abandon he leaped high into the air, snatching the leaf in his jaws and crunching it with canine glee.

The only thing that would be better would be if a dog, coyote or wolf showed up. He imagined sniffing its butt. Oh, what wonders. What bliss! There was so much to be learned about the world if people would only realize that the message is in the butt.

Wait, another tree. It must be marked! He spit out the leaf, lifted his leg again and squirted a bit of juice on it. Another tree for his collection.

Something broke from cover and darted through a bush.

He couldn't see it very well, but his nose immediately put a name to the object.

A rabbit.

Trug's golden eyes went wide and he thundered after the rabbit.

Chapter 2

The vampire-trainee frowned in concentration and shifted his hands behind the girl's neck. He opened his mouth wide and …

Got slapped on the back of the head.

"Idiot! It's not a hunk of rawhide. You'll bruise it if you just masticate it."

"Masticate?"

"Chew, you moron. What do they teach you in schools, nowadays? Anyway, you must treat it like a very ripe fruit. Just let your fang slide into the jugular and let the fluid flow to you. We are not savages … like werewolves." The last words were snarled.

The newly Undead obediently lowered his head to the exposed white neck. As he approached the juicy, throbbing vein, a pool of drool leaked from his mouth onto the pearly skin. He braced himself for another head slap.

Instead, the captive girl began weakly struggling.

"You're losing her," the Master said. "Get your glamour back."

"My what?"

Another slap, "Your glamour!"

"Oh, that hypnotizing thingy?"

The old vampire sighed. "Yes, that 'hypnotizing thingy."

He thought ruefully that young vampires were like green belts in karate. They have the talent, but their lack of control made them dangerous.

The young vampire leaned over the girl's face and stared into her eyes. The void of his black eyes seemed to draw the blue from her eyes like a mini-black hole. Her lids drooped as she relaxed again.

"Very good, young cub, now back to the feeding."

Excitement mounting, the young vampire leaned in at an angle that popped his neck vertebra. As his lips gently kissed the young girl's velvet skin, sharp white fangs grew to nasty lethalness and slid into her neck.

Suddenly one of her hands shot out, slammed into his face and she bolted upright.

"Jerk! We're just practicing! You aren't supposed to really bite!"

"I'm sorr-rry," he stammered.

Winifred smoothed her dress, "Do you know how hard it was to make my blood pump like a normal human!"

"I said I was sorry," the vampire wouldn't meet her eyes.

She turned to the old vampire, while peeling the blue contact lenses from her eyes, "Seriously, if your little boys can't control themselves, you can just find yourself another 'victim."

With an athletic move that would have earned her at least a bronze in the Olympics, she vaulted to her feet and stormed out of the room, her walk somehow managing to combine predator and sexiness in delicious amounts.

The Master and his protégé were mesmerized by her swaying departure. They might be dead, but they were still guys.

She went into a room and the door slammed behind her.

The two vampires stared at the spot, imprinting the memory. After the moment was exhausted, the Master held out a banana.

"What's that?" the young vampire asked.

"A banana. You will practice on this."

"Aw! That's gross. You know I can't eat normal food anymore."

"The better to make sure you are careful in your lessons, young cub. Try not to bruise it."

With that, the Master vampire faded to mist.

Chapter 3

There are reasons butterflies and rabbits move erratically. Each of them spends much of its life trying to avoid something that wants to eat it.

Nevin the rabbit raced under low hanging branches and vaulted over stumps, juking right and left, double-juking, triple-juking, his eyes bulging with fear. His respiration would have rivaled a hummingbird on caffeine.

Behind him a huge wolf-like shape bounded in pursuit, bushy tail compensating on the turns.

Nevin hadn't been chased like this since the janitor at the community pool caught him peeking in the girl's locker room. He still suspected most of the janitor's anger was because Nevin was butting in on the janitor's own favorite pastime.

If there hadn't been a big dog ravening on his butt, Nevin probably would be trying to figure out why he was a rabbit, and what he was doing in these woods. But with a hot savage wolf panting on his cotton tail, all Nevin could think of was to run as fast as his four legs could take him.

His eyesight and hearing were remarkable and though he was racing at an amazing pace, Nevin felt in command of his wild gyrating through the woods. Even as he bounced left and right, he searched for a safe little hidey-hole to duck into.

There was a rocky hill ahead with loose shale, and Nevin scampered over the rocks with the alacrity of … well … a rabbit.

If he hadn't been running for his life, he would have enjoyed some mirth at the panicked scrabbling sound of the wolf losing its footing in the shale. But he was too busy looking for an escape route.

He zipped over the top of the hill and beheld something that normally would cause him dismay.

High school.

Now though, it was the perfect refuge. He knew its nooks and crannies as well as any student …

… student … huh … but he's a rabbit.

He shook his head in confusion and got back to the business of avoiding becoming Kibbles and Bits.

The sound of a wolf chuffing up the shale behind him was a timely reminder of his plight.

Without further thought, he scampered down the hill.

Unfortunately, while his light frame made him a better climber than the wolf, the wolf's bulk and longer legs aided it on downhill sprints.

A looming shadow was the only warning Nevin received. Fortunately, it was the only one he needed. With finely honed rabbit reflexes, he darted to the right without loss of speed, and was rewarded by the buffet of the wolf blowing right past. The wolf snarled in frustration as it tried to halt its forward momentum.

Nevin angled downhill, trying to reduce the wolf's advantage of gravity and momentum. He risked a glance and saw his pursuer was back in full chase. Perversely, Nevin slowed, letting the wolf close.

A wide dog smile grew across the wolf's face when he saw his prey slowing. A wolf can outrun deer if given enough terrain, and the rabbit was obviously tiring.

254

Nevin was in fact getting winded. His path was diagonal to the building he had selected for his escape route. It was the gymnasium door, left open on this sunny day to let the smell of sweat socks blow out of the doors. Nevin knew his way around the gym.

The wolf pounded closer and Nevin slowed even more.

Suddenly, Nevin stopped and turned, raising onto his haunches. His furry chest heaved as tiny lungs pumped air furiously. He twitched his nose at the onrushing wolf and his whiskers whirred. The gym door yawned only about twenty yards away, but Nevin could see there was no way he could get there before the wolf.

With a look of triumph, the wolf raced towards him, intent on snatching him in his long jaws.

There are very few animals with the zero to full speed acceleration of a rabbit, and Nevin used every bit of this gift.

Like a little furry heat-seeking missile, he zipped directly at the wolf.

At the sight of its prey running at it, the wolf skidded to a stop in stunned amazement. Helpless jaws snapped as the rabbit dipped left and cut behind the wolf like an All-Pro halfback. The wolf spun around in confusion as Nevin sprinted … well … hopped … towards the gymnasium door. Before the wolf could recover, Nevin was inside.

Nevin tore through the gym, tiny claws clicking on the parquet floor. He cocked a long ear and could hear the wolf thunder into the building.

When he saw Nevin, the wolf veered sharply, golden eyes gleaming hotly in the empty room.

Nevin saw the room he wanted and bolted towards it. He could read the sign and if the wolf hadn't been chasing him, he might have pondered the fact that a rabbit could read English. Or anything for that matter.

But this was an opportunity he couldn't ignore.

The girl's locker room.

Naked girls.

Boo-yah!

With his little brain clouded with visions of female nudity, he didn't notice the wolf had taken a more direct route, and would intercept him before he made it to the room.

Fortunately, he was saved by the janitor.

Just before the wolf would have taken his head off, Nevin's finely honed prey instincts kicked into gear and he zigged to the wolf's zag. The wolf overshot and tried to brake on a floor that had just been cleaned, polished and shined by a janitor who took his job seriously.

If it hadn't been for fur, the wolf would have had rug burns down his entire flank. As it was, he skidded for twenty feet, claws scratching frantically.

Nevin somehow kept his balance, bounded into the locker room, and looked around- eyes on both sides of his head – another weird thing. He was on the lookout for a wonderfully curvy, naked female human form. Again, he managed to ignore the fact that he was of an entirely different species.

No one. The locker room was deserted.

He blew out a rabbit sigh of disappointment just as the wolf lurched into the locker room.

Nevin whipped around and headed through the showers towards the other door. As he came around the corner of the lockers he sucked in the heady aroma of perfume and other girly scents... but wait ... no time, no time! Must run!

He looked at the door going to the hallways.

Locked!

Well, maybe not locked. But it was closed, and he was way too short to reach the doorknob. That and the lack of opposable thumbs would defeat any attempts to unlock a door.

He was trapped.

The wolf's feet clicked on the tile floor and Nevin hoped that the wolf was dumb enough to be fooled again.

Nevin bounded around the locker and encountered the wolf just as he was going through the shower. Water puddled on the floor from the end of the last class or athletic event. As Nevin rushed towards the hunter, the wolf stopped, braced both feet, and readied himself to gobble up a rabbit tidbit if he tried to trick it again.

Uh, oh. This wolf wasn't dumb.

Crap.

At the last moment, Nevin tried to change his direction, but the tiles were too slick. He slipped onto his side and went into an uncontrolled slide. So instead of running into ready jaws, he slid sideways under a very surprised wolf who just managed to nip off a bit of rabbit tail.

Nevin scrambled to his feet and ran back towards the exit.

This time, he ran for the boy's locker room, the wolf snapping at his heels.

Nevin had an escape route planned, but he hadn't counted on closed doors. Strangely, until this moment, the question whether a door was open or closed hadn't seemed like much of an obstacle.

The Coach's office was closed. Nevin spared a moment for a rabbit curse. Then he dipped around a cart of basketballs and hopped towards the showers. The wolf was done being subtle and simply crashed through the cart, scattering Spaulding stuff all over the room.

The balls were bigger than Nevin, so he couldn't risk getting hit. Zipping through and around the bounding balls, he headed towards the locker room conference officials used when officiating basketball and volleyball games. He sprinted into the room, only to find there was no exit.

There was only one hiding place. A pile of dirty, smelly, sweat stained clothes.

The choice? Hide in the laundry and hope the stinky boy smell was so foul it would defeat the olfactory senses of a wolf?

Or?

He looked back at the laundry. A yellowish jock strap beckoned him with demon glee. From the open doorway, he could hear the sounds of an irritated wolf tripping over basketballs. He looked back at the laundry, and made his decision.

The wolf rounded the corner, panting with frustration. Its long wicked fangs gleamed yellow in the dim light.

Nevin the rabbit attacked.

(download onto ebook in just minutes by going to www.normcowie.com and clicking the Buy link.

Norm's books

http://www.normcowie.com

Bonk & Hedz ... a caveman ... and woman ... story

Bonk and his mate Hedz are just an ordinary caveman and cavewoman struggling with the everyday existence that comes when one's place in the food chain isn't all that clear. Then a little caveman shows up and convinces them a neighboring tribe is amassing weapons of mass destruction in preparation for an assault on their village, and everything changes...with hilarious results.

The Adventures of Guy

Somebody stole Seth's brain, not that he was using it anyway. To recover it, his brother Guy and college roommates Knob and Thurman must take on sinister forces using only their wits, knowledge of beer and an Amazon Warrior, whose breasts, like the Big Gulp, are too big for the cup holder. "Humorous fantasy at its best..." Armchair Interviews. Named a "Top Ten Novel of the Year" Pop Syndicate

The Next Adventures of Guy

Every "Quest" has to have a sorcerer, an elf, a warrior, special effects...and most of all, a sequel. So in the hilarious sequel to The Adventures of Guy, Guy and his college buddies, Knob and Thurman, take on a new quest...to save Earth from alien invasion. Winner of Preditors and Editors Readers Choice award for Best Sci-fi fantasy.

Fang Face

Erin has been bitten twice by a vampire, and is turning into an Undead with a taste for blood smoothies. Her friends and family decide they like her more as normal teen, so they gear up to protect her from the third bite that will turn her into a coffin sleeper forever. "I loved this book, fangs and all," New York Times best-selling author James Rollins "Fantastically funny," BookLoons "Don't miss this gem," Shane Gericke, national best-selling author. "...genuinely funny..." Taliesin - The Vampire's Lair. Five-starred by Amazon top reviewer Harriet Klausner.

WereWoof

Two teens-turned-weredogs use their newfound powers of Kibbles and Bits to battle turncoat werewolves and bloodsucking vampires and save their friend from the pointy toothed villains. A stand-alone sequel to Fang Face. "...clever one-liners..." Constance Hullander, author of Snowstorm. "Like a fun vacation..." Ophelia Julien, author of Saving Jake

The Guy'd Book ... why we leave the seat ... and other stuff

A tongue in cheek training manual for women so they can understand what makes guys guys. Why we leave the toilet seat up, why we will do anything on a dare ... essentially, what makes us tick. Fun stuff previously published in the Chicago Tribune, Cynic Magazine and other places. Brought to you in beautiful black and white by award-winning author Norm Cowie. "A hilarious piece of work..." Scott Doornbosch, author of Basic Black

And short Adventures of Guy stories in the anthologies:

The Heat of the Moment

Missing

Some of Norm's reviews:

on Fang Face and its sequel WereWoof

"I loved this book, fangs and all." ~ Best selling author James
Rollins
"... fantastically funny." ~ BookLoons
"This book sucks ... in a most delightful way. Don't miss this
gem.." ~ Shane Gericke, national bestselling author
"... an amusing teen vampire tale..." ~ Five-starred review ~
Harriet Klausner, Amazon's #1 book reviewer
"...genuinely funny..." ~ Taliesin - The Vampire's Lair

on The Adventures of Guy and its sequel The Next Adventures of Guy

"... humorous fantasy at its best..." ~ Armchair Interviews
(Amazon Top reviewer)
"...LOL funny" ~ Beverly at Publisher's Weekly
"No topic is safe from Cowie's incredible wit and entertaining
turn-of-phrase." ~ Pop Syndicate (named one of Pop Syndicate's Top
Ten Books of 2007)
"...hilarious mishaps...." ~ Joliet Herald News
"Hilarious, witty and oozing with snappy sarcasm..." ~3Rs Bits,
Bites & Books
"Don't bother picking up this one if you've no sense of humor"
~
Amanda Richards, Amazon Top Reviewer
"Everything in the book is so true, you can't help but laugh in
agreement." ~ Roundtable Reviews
The Next Adventures of Guy, winner "Best Sci-Fi Fantasy" in
Preditors and Editors readers choice award

Proof

Made in the USA
Charleston, SC
19 September 2011